CW01502150

Power of the Sea

Dangerous Waters

by
Eileen Josephine Bilton

1663 LIBERTY DRIVE, SUITE 200
BLOOMINGTON, INDIANA 47403
(800) 839-8640
WWW.AUTHORHOUSE.COM

First published by AuthorHouse 10/26/05

ISBN: 1-4208-8441-7 (sc)

Printed in the United States of America
Bloomington, Indiana

This book is printed on acid-free paper.

Fishermen's Prayer

The young man knocked on the pearly gates

And a voice called from inside

'Who is that who disturbs my peace?'

And the fisherman replied,

'My time has come to join you but do I pay a fee

To make my upward journey from down beneath the sea?'

'There's nought you owe' the Saint replied

'Your dues you've paid in full

In sweat and blood on frozen seas

And storms you battled through.'

A harp he passed to the fisherman and
said, 'Go rest your weary feet

A different welcome it will be when I the Owners meet.'

Chapter 1

His innards rose and fell in rhythm with the violent rolling motion of the vessel as he tried to take in the shock of what he had just witnessed. Andy Pattison had seen many accidents on board trawlers but never one so horrific. Bill had been a good mate to him; always generous, rarely had a bad word to say about anyone. He would be sorely missed.

The young man had had no time to fear for his life. With the precision and swiftness of a highly skilled surgeon, a parted warp had decapitated Bill without mercy, cleanly separating his head from its resting place above the broad shoulders. The icy wind had mockingly cauterised the wound around the exposed vertebrae to guard against infection. There was little blood to be seen; little evidence of the heinous act as the angry ocean relentlessly sterilised the slippery deck. The proud head had served its owner well for twenty-six years.

Andy forgot the nauseating stench of gutted fish and oil, which penetrated everywhere above and below deck; and the mountainous waves sweeping across the bow, determined to grasp another victim. But, he would carry with him forever the memory of Bill's cruel and untimely end. He turned to make his way below deck, battling against the ferocious wind, which continued to inflame the ocean's insatiable appetite. This time it was left wanting.

Over the next two days the blizzards continued to prevail, increasing and decreasing with no real pattern. A rare glimpse of daylight helped to raise the spirits of the embattled crew of the *St Helena* but everyone was exhausted. The continual struggle to hold back the heavy build-up of ice on the superstructure was taking its toll on everyone: axes, hammers, anything handy was used to try to keep the ice to a minimum, including hot water hoses when possible. The radio platform had to be kept clear; the bosun and his watch took turns to climb the slippery ladder, desperately holding on to each other's legs for safety. But, everyone knew that there could ultimately be only one winner in this war.

Early on the third day, still struggling to win the battle against the extreme weather conditions, the skipper gave orders from the bridge to shoot the gear into the eye of the storm. The crew argued with him; it was far too risky an operation. It would be better and far safer to wait until the weather improved. Even then, the operation would still be highly dangerous.

With the initial shock of Bill's demise subsiding, the mutterings amongst the men were becoming increasingly angry and insistent. Soon, when the battle against the elements was diminishing, and there was time to reflect, they would demand an answer; why did it happen? At the moment, the men's priorities lay with the gruelling tasks demanding to be done. The skipper would have to live with Bill Johnson's blood on his hands for the rest of his life. Who would envy him that? There were those on board who doubted whether he cared. After all, he was fully aware of what can happen in such severe weather conditions, especially if a wrong decision is taken. His certificates were proof of his competence and knowledge. He knew that heavy seas can push the hull into the winch seriously affecting the tension of the warps running off the winch drums; it can cause the warps to part, injuring or killing someone. Bill Johnson was testament to that. And, the trawl doors can be severely damaged by the elements; they can fall flat and fly off their allotted course, amputating body parts, or pushing men overboard. On rare occasions, a man would be washed back onto the deck. He would be lucky. But, just as quickly, the waves can snatch back what is rightfully theirs. He is not so lucky then.

The Old Man's decision that morning to fish on the opposite side of the bow, knowing that the trawler would be pushed across its own warps was insane. But, he had been hell-bent on trying for the last haul, ignoring the prevailing weather conditions. Not many skippers would risk their ship's and their crew's lives with such abandonment. But, he was the boss; his orders had to be obeyed. And his calculations were usually right.

The Arctic weather is a cruel adversary. Ethereal pillars of ice tantalise the landscape, flitting in and out of the blizzards like the amorphous lost souls of those who had perished in the ocean's depths. The fishermen are never deceived by an iceberg's alluring beauty. They know that hidden below the surface of the dark water, the ice maidens linger, hungrily. In the winter, when daylight comes for only one hour in twenty-four, and the fishermen's only friends are the hungry gulls, the men's most dangerous opponents are the icebergs. Yet, they stoically accept the harsh and hazardous environment knowing that their lives will not be their own until they safely return to the sanctity of their homes. Family comforts are theirs for only a short time; unless they lose their jobs.

The prospect of having no money was a far greater worry to the trawlermen than the dangerous life they led at sea.

Many of them boozed and gambled away what was left of their hard-earned bonuses after their womenfolk have been given their share. They travelled from one pub or club to another in taxis. Their courage was never questioned by the landlords, who envied the men's 'here today, gone tomorrow' philosophy.

'Do womenfolk up and down the country ever spare a thought for the dangers we have to face in order to catch the fish that ends up on their dinner table?' an angry voice would ask. But was not that anger justified? 'They can't be blamed for something they know nowt about,' someone else would point out. But, fishermen's widows knew only too well the sacrifice that had to be made in order to catch the fish.

'*An*d what about the bloody owners?' The question was a frequent topic of conversation, as the fishermen sat in the pub with a pint in front of them; or perhaps, in the ship's mess at mealtimes. 'How many really care what we have to go through to keep the bloody gaffers' pockets lined, their cars in their drives and their womenfolk in fur coats?' The laments were always the same.

As Andy lay in his bunk trying to ignore the heavy roll of the ship and the noise from the engines below, he thought of the dead man's wife and small son, Ronnie, with another one due in a month's time; another mouth to feed. The Pastor of the Fishermen's Bethel, the purveyor of bad news, would never be out of a job; a listening ear and a shoulder to cry on were always available, no matter what time of the day or night comfort was needed, Andy thought, cynically.

Once again, he felt the bile rising in his throat. Rest was impossible. Bill Johnson's death had been so sudden; so horrendous. The sight of the young man's head disappearing into the ocean's foaming belly was graphically imprinted on Andy's mind; he still saw the huge wave, its curved sweeping tip a shimmering mass of icy glass beads, greedily devouring its prey. The headless body seemed to hover for a moment in shock before disappearing into the depths of the sea. Was it, perhaps, making a pointless effort to become whole again? Maybe, in another life...

Andy longed for the comfort and safety of his bed at home; and the warm feeling of Maggie's arms around him as they sat cuddling on the back row of the pictures. They were soon to be married; a Christmas wedding. The last time he was home he had promised her he would look for a shore job - but as what? There were few jobs to be had. He sighed deeply. Sleep eluded him, yet he was exhausted both mentally and physically.

Suddenly he felt the ship lurch violently. The terrifying sounds of splintering wood and crushing metal rent the air. The vessel was plunged into darkness. Its superstructure was no match for the mountain of ice as it defended its territory. Men and objects were flung around the confined spaces of the small trawler, crashing them into the wooden side panels without compassion. The men in the engine room had no chance against the havoc being wreaked against them. Their screams went unheeded as boiling steam gushed from broken and misplaced pipes stripping the skin from their flesh.

For a fleeting moment, Andy thought of Maggie and his heart wept.

———

The City of Hull was in mourning, yet again; another trawler lying at the bottom of a watery graveyard, the roles of hunter and the hunted reversed; eyes of brave young men left to stare in shock as they peered lifelessly through the murky black waters that filled the broken hulk, which had been the men's home for almost two weeks. There had been no time for anyone to send messages to family and loved ones, who would be waiting for them to return home. There would be no bodies to confirm who the men were who had died, which would have allowed the bereaved to come to terms properly with their grief; only the company's records of the crew's names could be taken as proof of their having been on board the *St Helena*. There would be no graves to sit by and pass on news of little Jimmy's first day at school, or Johnny Smith's latest run-in with the law.

The city's anger, shock and sadness was almost tangible.

Maggie was inconsolable. Her white velvet wedding dress hung in the old oak wardrobe standing in a corner of her bedroom. The long white veil, with its delicate tiara interwoven with sprigs of holly and red berries, lay neatly wrapped in tissue paper in a drawer of the dressing table. But, as the days passed, Maggie's grief changed to fury. The trawler owners were sitting pretty on their swelling bank balances, whilst their crews were dicing with death at the fishing grounds. If the ships made a loss, the owners could ride it. The trawlermen, on the other hand, would arrive home knowing, that the settling pot would be empty. The bills for their bond expenses still had to be paid; it was not right. Things had to change.

Less than two weeks later, tragedy struck yet again. The *Lamorna* sank in thick fog on skerries off Southern Greenland. One man was saved.

It would have been Andy's twenty-first birthday that day. He and Maggie had been children when they first met, his friendly, blue eyes locking on to Maggie's unhappy gaze as they stood in Paragon Station with their cardboard suitcases and their gasmasks. The country was at war once again. Andy told her later that that was the moment he first knew that one day he would marry her.

Chapter 2 (1941)

———————————

'Look, Maggie. There's Keith and Pat. Wave to them.' John pointed to two children about their own age who were standing further along the platform.

Maggie was not interested. 'I want my mam.'

"Don't leave go of my hand or you'll get lost." Her brother John's warning was almost lost in the cacophony of voices on the platform and the sound of the train's engine.

Martha Bell was standing on the sidelines, head held high, showing no emotion; but that was Martha. It was evacuation day and only the organisers knew the children's final destinations; it was a secret.

Preparations to evacuate the children, and their mothers too, if they wished to be included, had meticulously been put in place over recent months. Few people believed that the war with Germany would soon be over. The Greeks had surrendered, the Low Countries fallen, and France and Germany had agreed an armistice. Other nations were desperately trying to hold on to their freedom and independence. But, Hitler had a dream to fulfil.

Nine months ago, he had claimed his first victims in Hull. Hundreds of people had died or were injured by low-flying German aircrafts, when they had bombarded the city for two nights at the beginning of May. Everyone knew someone, or of someone, who had been affected by the blitz and the citizens knew that that was only the beginning. Homes and shops lay in ruins from those first air raids. The centre of the city was devastated; Control Headquarters destroyed; essential services badly affected. Then, before the city had fully come to terms with what had happened, it was once again faced with the might of Hitler's wrath; still, the brave people of Hull were determined not to give in to the oppressors. The inherent fear that tragedy can strike at any time had lived with them for hundreds of years. After all, deep-sea fishing was in their blood.

Maggie clasped John's hand tightly as they stood together on the station platform. The continual bombing at night had frightened her but she would much rather remain at home with her mother and other brother, Alan; did her and John really need to go away to the country? To somewhere nice, they had been told. Alan was sick with TB. Maggie knew that he was very poorly; something serious. He would sometimes cough up blood. He always told her it was nothing to worry about; she had no reason to disbelieve him.

She was used to her dad being away for long periods; he was a deep-sea fisherman. It always seemed like Christmas when he came home. She always knew what she would find when she delved into the hidden depths of his kitbag: Quality Street, tins of salmon and crayfish. The last time she saw him he was wearing a smart, dark uniform; it seemed a long time ago. Her mother had told her, 'Daddy's in the Navy. He's a sailor.' Maggie was not sure what that really meant; but it must be something to do with fishing because he could be away for a long time. She was certain that, when he came back, he would collect her and John from the country and take them home; he loved them. Her mother was sending them away, so she did not care.

Maggie allowed her gaze to wander aimlessly around the crowded platform. She recognised a number of children. Some were upset, one or two looked withdrawn and bewildered; others were obviously excited at the thought of a holiday in the country. Each child carried a box supported on one shoulder by a belt or a strong piece of string. The cloying odour of rubber betrayed their contents; gasmasks. They were essential; but everyone hoped that they would never need to be used. Children's clothing had been hurriedly packed into carrier bags or cardboard suitcases; two of everything. Hopefully, favourite toys had been included, to bring comfort during the long days and nights away from familiar surroundings and family back in Hull. Mothers had been instructed to give their children packs of sandwiches, as it could be a long time before they were given a meal. Maggie and John had a choice of jam or dripping. Fruit was practically non-existent although, sometimes, it was possible to buy half an orange for a halfpenny, the other half of the fruit having been discarded because it was rotten. Every child's ration book and milk tokens were safely hidden at the bottom of their bags; or should be. Name badges pinned to the children's coats were perhaps more important than anything.

Maggie noticed a boy about John's age watching her from a few yards away. He had blonde, curly hair. He looked nice. She averted her eyes.

'Pat and Keith are coming to join us,' said John. The girl was waving frantically. But Maggie looked at her without smiling before turning her gaze towards some obscure point on the ground.

Pat was a few months older than Maggie although they were in the same class at school; they lived in adjacent streets and had been friends since they were toddlers. Maggie was not normally as lively and confident as her friend; she was quiet and shy. But when the two girls were together, she giggled a lot and was very chatty. Pat was the younger of Freda and Tom Walker's two children and very different in character to her brother, Keith; he could be sullen and possessive. Tom had been excused from war duty; he suffered from asthma. One or two of their neighbours questioned this. Their husbands and sons had had to go to war, why not Tom Walker? He wasn't really an invalid.

'Aren't you excited, Maggie?' Pat asked her friend.

'No. I don't want to leave my mam.' Maggie started to cry again then wiped her nose on her coat sleeve.

'But, it's not for ever,' pointed out Pat. 'And your mam will come to see you.'

Maggie's face brightened.

'Please stop talking everyone and listen carefully,' commanded an authoritative voice over a microphone. Its owner was a lady in the Women's Voluntary Service, dressed in the regulatory green skirt, matching jacket, and hat adorned with a WVS badge. 'My name is Mrs Suddaby. Before getting on the train, you will all be put into small groups. It is most important that you remember which party you are with or you could get lost.'

John squeezed Maggie's hand protectively.

It took over an hour to organise the children into pre-arranged groups of fifteen, together with a few mothers and infants who were joining them. Maggie was relieved to know that her and John had been grouped with Pat and Keith. Then she noticed the blonde haired boy again. He was standing a few feet away talking to another boy about the same age as himself. He saw Maggie and smiled at her. Shyly, she looked away from him, still without a smile. She didn't know him.

'Quiet, please, everyone.' Mrs Suddaby's voice rose once again above the noise of the engine and the incessant chattering around her. 'I'm sure you will all enjoy your visit to the country.' A visit did not imply permanence. 'Will you please now get on the train as quickly as possible. It would be appreciated if all those people not travelling with the children would leave the platform immediately. Thank you.'

Keith moved possessively closer to Maggie, as their group walked over to the train. He stood behind her, waiting for her to board. As she stepped off the platform, a hand reached out from above to help her. She looked up. It belonged to the blonde boy she had seen earlier on the platform. He was smiling at her again. He had got on the train before her and was standing in the doorway. She allowed him to help her safely aboard. He turned without speaking and made his way into one of the carriages. Keith glared at his departing figure.

An hour and a half later, the train reached its destination, Tibthorne on the Wolds: somewhere nice in the country. The children had stared fascinated on their journey at rabbits and hares running freely in the fields. Normally, they were to be seen in cages or served on dinner plates next to dollops of potato, peas and carrots; their skins were made into gloves to keep hands warm during the cold, dark days of winter. Nothing was ever wasted.

After the children were lined up in front of the Church Hall, various members of the village walked up and down the rows; to choose a child or children they would be responsible for, on a temporary basis only; until the authorities decided that it was safe for the youngsters to return home. The operation was rather like a cattle market, trading in children rather than cows or pigs.

'You can come with me,' said a rather plump lady, smiling through spectacles at Maggie and John. Her long dark hair had been woven into plaits, which were pinned to the top of her head. Her face was round with the pink, healthy glow of country life. 'You can come too,' she added, looking at the blonde boy who was now standing nearby on his own.

'No, you can't take him,' Keith interrupted quickly. 'My sister and me are with them. Our mams want us to stay together.'

'I'm very sorry, my love, but I can only take three of you,' the lady explained, apologetically. She turned to the blonde boy. 'Pick up your things, lad, then all of you follow me.'

Chapter 3 (1959)

'When's it due, lass? You didn't think you could hide it for ever, did you?' Martha stared at her daughter, her large, imposing frame hovering over the bed.

Maggie did not answer. Her face was white and drawn; any sense of shame she felt was hidden in the luminous depths of her sea-green eyes; the paleness of her skin accentuated their colour.

'You've got two choices, as far as I can see. You can marry Keith and not tell him about your condition until you've been married a few weeks; let him think it's his. Or, you could go away somewhere and have the bairn, then put it up for adoption afterwards. If you choose the first option, can you live with your conscience?'

There was no mention of an abortion, Maggie noticed. She had heard stories about people who did them; some girls died. She remained silent.

'There's no way your dad's going to accept a bastard in his house.' Martha paused. 'Think about what I've said. If you decide to have it adopted, you can go to our Nora's at Beverley 'til it's all over. I'll tell your dad she's sick and you're looking after her. He won't like it but that won't matter. He's away most of the time. And he certainly won't think of visiting you at our Nora's. He can't stand her.'

As Martha prepared to leave the room, her old, worn slippers treading silently on the cold bare canvass, she turned and looked at her daughter again. 'You got yourself into this mess, now you've got to get yourself out of it.' Holding the doorknob in her hand, for a moment longer than necessary, she added, 'Everything will be all right, lass.'

Martha was a complex person; hard and unyielding on the outside but with an underlying sense of compassion. It had been suggested by Nora, on more than one occasion, that Martha feared the vulnerability that comes when feelings are exposed.

Like other fishermen's wives, Martha had struggled to bring up her children on her own. She had travelled the sorrowful, lonely days of bereavement whilst her husband was at sea. Alan was only twenty-one years old when he died of tuberculosis. She had preyed to God every night, sometimes more than once, that her other two children would be saved from the same fate. TB was commonplace and often a killer; like diphtheria. So far, He had answered her prayers. But, deep-sea fishing could, and did, claim its own victims. John, now twenty-three years old, was currently fighting his own battle in the Barents Sea.

Sitting alone in her bedroom after Martha had left, Maggie pondered her mother's words. There was no way she would ever risk deceiving anyone about something as important as a baby; certainly, not Keith. Maggie was not a liar. Besides, he did not have a forgiving nature.

Maggie had shared her secret with Pat. That was what best friends were for. Maggie trusted her implicitly. Many times in the past, Pat had said that she lived in hope that her friend would marry Keith one day; she also insisted, when she knew about the baby, that she would never stand by and watch her brother being deceived, no matter how much sympathy she felt for her friend. Maggie respected her for that.

In any case, she felt sure that Keith could never come to love Andy's child and accept it as his own, no matter how much he cared about her and wanted to be with her. He had always loved her, even when they had been at school. But, his possessiveness towards her made her feel claustrophobic at times. He had stopped proposing to her soon after she became engaged to Andy. But his eyes betrayed his need for her whenever they were near to each other.

Maggie had watched his jealousy intensify, flourishing into the vitriolic hatred, which had controlled him up to the time of Andy's death. It had begun on a platform in Paragon Station on Evacuation Day; when they were so young. Within a few weeks of arriving at the farm, blonde haired Andy, who was living there with John and Maggie, was spending more and more time in his bedroom, withdrawn and often nursing bruises; they always seemed to appear after Keith and Pat had visited the farm. Andy always found excuses for the marks. Maggie had been too young to be able to help him then; but she had felt the undercurrents whenever the two boys were together.

Maggie buried herself in the colourful patchwork quilt as she lay on her bed. She remembered the scandal surrounding Ada Gibson. Ada had gone away for a few months last summer. Maggie had overheard Mrs Adamson, the local gossip who lived a few doors away from the Bell's house, telling Martha that Ada had 'got caught' and gone away to have IT. She had sneered. 'She's right flighty, that one. An oo'er. I wonder which one got her up the spout.' Maggie had felt sorry for Ada. Now, people would say the same about her.

She pondered the consequences if she decided to keep the baby. She could learn to cope with the gossip, she felt sure, but what about the child as it grew older? It would be referred to as 'Maggie Bell's bastard'. No matter how much she loved it, however well she cared for it, the baby would grow up with that stigma. She considered the option of having the baby adopted; but there could be no guarantee that anyone else would love and care for her child as much as she would. But, on the other hand, would her love be enough? She would need money to feed and clothe them both. If her father threw her out onto the streets, which was most probable, she would have to find somewhere for her and the baby to live; how would she pay the rent? She would have to work. How could she do that and look after a child?

The more Maggie considered her options the more distraught and confused she became. She thought again about her dad. He was sure to tell her that she was a slut if he found out she was pregnant. The fact that she was his favourite child would make no difference at all. Terry would rant and rave as if he had an unblemished past. Maggie had heard her mother call him 'woman fond' so often during a shouting match between the two of them, usually after he had been boozing. But when Terry's past was brought up he would retaliate by saying that men were different from women and, in any case, she was wrong about him and should not listen to vicious rumours. 'What about your sister, Nora?' The questions and answers thrown back and forth were always the same.. Maggie had tried on occasions to find out what Nora was supposed to have done. 'Mind your own business. Children should be seen and not heard.' Maggie was no longer a child but still received the same answer from Martha.

For a moment, Maggie hated her father. She knew that there was no way he would ever allow her to bring up an illegitimate child in his home; even though the baby she was carrying was his grandchild. And, after all, she had loved Andy very much and they were to have been married at Christmas. Surely that counted for a lot.

As she struggled to find answers to her problem, they seemed increasingly unsurmountable. And, whatever the outcome, there was going to be pain.

Maggie turned over and buried her face further in her pillow. Her thoughts turned to John. How would he react when he knew that she was pregnant? What would he say? Perhaps, he would be ashamed of her. But, he knew how much Andy had meant to her. In ten days' time, he would be home from sea; five tides, hardly enough time to visit her if she went to stay with Auntie Nora. But, if he felt embarrassed about her condition, it would give him a good excuse to stay away.

'What's the matter with our Maggie? The usual again, is it?'

Terry Bell's voice reached his daughter, as she stood at the top of the narrow, rickety stairs, which led to both the front door and the kitchen-cum-living room. There was no banister-rail to hold on to. If you missed your footing, you balanced yourself precariously as best you could, with one hand on the wall. Otherwise, you reached the small mat protecting the hallway in a somewhat undignified position; at worst, you would break your neck. Maggie realised that it provided another serious option for her to consider. It was a fleeting thought, but powerful. She made her way down the narrow staircase, her face flushed with embarrassment. She automatically steadied herself with one hand on the wall. As she neared the bottom, she heard her mother say, 'Shush'.

Maggie had been twelve years' old when 'the curse' had first presented itself. 'She's a little woman now,' her mother had announced to her husband when Maggie returned from the backyard toilet. The memory, the feeling of shame, had remained with her, vividly, since then. But for now, she had been given a reprieve from the belly cramps and home-made pads. But, life had been much less complicated then. If only she could go back in time.

Terry Bell had arrived home the day before. He was due to depart again tomorrow, for Greenland. Normally, Maggie dreaded him going away. There was always a real possibility he would not return, particularly at this time of the year. But, for now, the minutes and the hours were dragging by. She was catching the bus to Beverley on Monday morning.

Severe gales had brought havoc to Hull and the east coast over the last couple of days; chimneys demolished, hoardings torn down. In the Old Town around Lowgate, some cellars had flooded to five feet or more. If the atrocious weather continued, trawlers would not be able to leave port.

As Maggie entered the room, her father looked up from his dinner plate and smiled, chewing his food noisily. Normally, Maggie found it distasteful but today she felt no reaction as she watched him wipe his mouth on the sleeve of his old navy blue jumper.

'You're putting on weight, our Maggie,' he remarked.

'Too many goodies she's been eating,' Martha pointed out quickly.

Maggie made no comment as she sat down at the table.

'You're very quiet, lass,' Terry pointed out. 'Not worrying about money, are you?'

'No, dad,' Maggie replied. 'I've saved a bit up and Auntie Nora is going to give me some pocket money whilst I look after her.' Maggie did not look at him as she spoke. She hated lying. 'She owes me one. That's all you need to know,' Martha had told her daughter earlier. 'In any case, families should always stick together.'

Maggie had been touched and puzzled by her Aunt's apparent eagerness to have her stay in her home, knowing her niece's predicament. But, Nora had always been an enigma.

Maggie had left her job in McKenzie's fish factory the day before; she was now unemployed.

'To look after my sick auntie in Beverley,' she had explained to Kenneth McKenzie, when he had asked why she was leaving. Lying to a boss was different from lying to family and friends. Trawler owners did not deserve any respect, as far as the fish-house girls were concerned. Maggie had not dared to look at him; he might see the truth lurking in her eyes

'You have been a good worker, Miss Bell. There will be a job waiting here for you, if you want it when you return home.' His offer had seemed genuine but could he be trusted. Probably not, thought Maggie. Owners are all the same; no heart or conscience. She had forced herself to thank him then left his office.

Andy had lost his life on the *St Helena*. It had not belonged to the McKenzie's family; but what difference did that make. If she did go back to her old job, it would only be because she desperately needed the money. Hopefully, there would be other jobs available when she needed one.

It irked Maggie to have to admit it to herself, but she did not dislike Kenneth. He seemed a kind man. But, she hated his wife, Kathleen; the bitch in a fur coat, she was generally referred to in the fish-house. At the end of the day, the McKenzie family stood on the other side of the dividing line, living in their detached properties on the outskirts of Hull, travelling around in their elegant Ford cars; Kenneth's and Paul's were black, Kathleen's shiny red. Kathleen was a well-known figure in the city, always instantly recognised by her posh hats and fur coats; few people had a good word to say about her. The family was an intrinsic part of an elite community, whose wealth came from fish, and the blood and sweat of their employees.

However, the McKenzie workforce generally acknowledged, that the son, Paul, and his wife, Sara, always seemed genuinely interested in the workers; they never failed to greet the fish-house girls with friendliness and respect, showing none of the superiority displayed by Kathleen. But, they still belonged to the McKenzie family of trawler owners.

'What's the matter, lass, cat got your tongue?' Terry's voice brought Maggie's attention back to the dinner table and away from the McKenzie family. 'You're in a world of your own.'

She struggled to act normally in front of him; but she longed to be back in the sanctity of her bedroom. But, that would only bring more remarks and questions.

'It's not good for you, to mope around, lass,' Tom pointed out. 'Andy's not coming back and it's time you accepted the fact. Life goes on.'

It was the second time in two days that she had been told that; the first by Keith. Her anger, which until now, she had managed to keep tightly suppressed, exploded with volcanic fury. No longer could the intense heat simmering inside her be controlled. 'You men are all the same,' she shouted. 'You just sit back and accept your lot, whilst the owners sit pretty in their expensive houses counting their money.' Maggie's eyes blazed; her cheeks had turned a vivid shade of red. 'Why do you let the greedy bastards get away with it, dad?' she pleaded. She turned to her mother. 'Can't you do anything, mam, to make my dad see sense?'

Martha faced her daughter, angrily. 'There's nothing you can do so keep out of it. It's up to the men. It's not a woman's job to interfere.

'Then, maybe it's time it was, if the men are too bloody weak to face the bloody trawler owners,' Maggie shouted. She felt the stinging slap of her mother's hand across her face. An angry white weal intruded into the glowing red blush of her cheek. As she rushed to the door, she heard Martha calling after her, 'Don't you ever use that fish-house language again in this house, miss.'

It was all right for adults to swear but not their children; no matter how old they were and especially if they were still living in the family home. Expletives of the worst kind were normal, and accepted, on the trawlers. Away from the rest of society, and facing horrendous conditions at sea, the men had an excuse; a bit of self-control was exercised by the fishermen, when with their children. Most wives swore, one or two using dialect normally heard only on board ship. Then it was described as colourful, even funny sometimes; those women were characters in their own right. But they were also regarded as disgusting and common. Mrs Adamson, who had called Ada Gibson an oo'er, belonged to that category.

Maggie left the kitchen, banging the door behind her. As she made her way upstairs to her bedroom, she could hear her mother and father shouting at each other; debating their daughter's lack of respect for her elders. Once in her room, Maggie wrapped herself in the comforting seclusion of the patchwork quilt on her bed. As she lay there, her intense anger turned to sadness, then her tears started to flow. She was crying a lot nowadays.

Martha had patiently sewn the patchwork quilt by hand over many years, for Maggie's bottom drawer; it was the custom. But, that was when Andy was alive; she was going to be a Christmas bride. There were over two hundred pieces of colourful material in the cover, each telling a different story. Normally, Maggie never tired of looking at them in the dim light before she went to sleep at night. She would weave a story around any she could not identify with the family background. But, today, her mind was on other things.

How could so many men, who fought horrendous battles at the fishing grounds, even in the winter when the weather was at its worst, be so frightened of facing a small group of trawler owners and asking for justice. It did not make any sense to Maggie.

There was a light tap on the bedroom door. Maggie ignored it.

'Maggie, can I come in, lass? I want to talk to you.'

Without waiting for an answer, Martha opened the door. She walked across the room and sat on her daughter's bed. 'I'm sorry I hit you,' she said.

Maggie made no reply, nor did she look at her mother. She had no intention of apologising to her for swearing. She felt her anger rising again.

'It's not the men's fault, love,' Martha said.

'Of course, it is,' retorted Maggie. 'Why can't they stand up to the owners? Or, if they're too weak to do that, why don't the wives do something about it?'

'Like what?' Martha asked, quietly. 'Don't you realise that, it isn't only the ships that belong to the trawler owners, they own everything else as well, right down to the barrows on the docks. Your dad, and John, are part of all that. Their livelihoods, their lives, belong to the gaffers.'

Although Maggie could see the extent of the problem, she opened her mouth to argue again. There must be something that could be done to change things.

'Hear me out, lass,' insisted Martha. 'If a member of the crew complain in any way, or even if their face doesn't fit, they're out on their necks, sacked; sent on walkabouts. The word gets around and nobody will take them on. The gaffers make sure of that. No work, no pay. It's as simple as that. Even the skippers' jobs aren't safe, lass. Nobody can live without money. We all know that.'

Maggie's thoughts returned fleetingly to her own predicament. That would not last forever. But, unless something was done to change things, the trawler owners would continue to thrive on the blood of others.

'I still say it's the men's own fault,' Maggie argued. 'If they all ganged up together and refused to sail, the trawlers would not be able to be put to sea. The bosses would lose money. They would have to give in to the men.'

'Yes, but who would end up with an empty pocket; certainly not the owners. You've got a lot to learn, lass. And, remember you've got a bairn to think about now. Have you decided what you're going to do?'

Maggie remained silent. Martha shook her head and left the room.

———

Terry made his way downstairs as quietly as the creaking steps would allow. It was two o'clock in the morning. A light tapping on the door heralded the arrival of his taxi. He left the house without looking back; it was considered to be unlucky. As he walked down the terrace towards the waiting vehicle, his footsteps echoed on the icy concrete. The noise of the car's engine in the cold, clinging mist, soon faded into the distance.

Nobody had watched Terry depart; no quick kiss or affectionate wave had wished him farewell. He had packed his kitbag himself; nothing had been removed from it, nor would be, until the ship left the dockside. It should have been washday for Martha but it would have to wait; superstition dictated that a fisherman would be washed away if the rules were broken.

Maggie prayed for her father's safe return in three weeks' time. She would not want his death on her conscience. It would be quite a while before she saw him again. In a few hours' time, she would be on the bus to Beverley.

———

Martha and her sister, Nora, had never been particularly close but they had always sent each other birthday and

Christmas cards. And Martha had made sure that she visited her sister two or three times a year; Nora was not welcome in Terry Bell's home. Maggie never asked why; there was no point. She knew that she would never be given an honest answer. It was the community rule that families stood together whatever life threw at them. The Bells obviously had not adhered to those rules. Nora was an outcast as far as Terry Bell was concerned.

Yesterday, knowing that her husband would be going back to sea in a few hours and would have little time to argue with her, Martha told him that Nora was very ill and needed some help; Maggie was going to stay with her for a while. Tom accepted the situation reluctantly but said that Maggie could go, but only for as long as was necessary.

Nora was a widow, living in Beverley. She had married Billie Foster, a butcher, when she was twenty and he twenty-three; he was working in the family business. 'She's only marrying him to get away from Hessle Road. Too big for her boots, that's what she is,' Martha was heard to say, at the time; but not when her sister was around. But, Nora had never made any secret of the fact that she had hated living on Hessle Road, where she was brought up. The family home had been a small back-to-back terraced house in Edlington Street; no running water in the house; lavatory across the backyard with no light, the spiders allowed to reside openly in all the corners of the small cold room, to stop people lingering too long. Nora had always had an ambition to live in a large house with three bedrooms on the outskirts of the city. And, that was what she got.

During the early part of the war, there had been gossip about Nora. The story was that, while Billy was slogging his guts out, fighting the 'jerries' somewhere in France, she was having a good time. A few months after Billy was reported missing in action, presumed dead, Nora had admitted to

Martha that she had never really loved her husband. But she had never wished him dead, either.

'Live for today' had always been an unspoken sentiment within the fishing community. The city had seen much suffering over the years; severe bombardments during the war with hundreds of people killed, and one after another tragedies at sea, trawling being the city's main industry. But, most people accepted that none of these reasons should be used as an excuse for infidelity, however difficult life might be. Loneliness and fear had to be lived with. 'The devil always catches up with sinners,' Martha had warned her sister; but she had kept her secret safe. Now that debt needed to be repaid and she knew that her sister was not in a position to refuse.

But, Nora had always been very fond of Maggie, even though she did not see her very often. As far as Nora's neighbours were concerned, Maggie was a young widow, whose husband had been killed at sea off the Norwegian coast; a torpedo had exploded into the side of the ship on which he was serving. Maggie was three months' pregnant, at the time; a tragedy of war. It was not far from the truth. Deep-sea fishing has always been a kind of war; a battle against the harsh and hazardous elements in the Arctic waters.

———————

Maggie's stay with her aunt was a mixture of happiness and sadness; and also one of enlightenment.

One evening, as they both sat knitting in front of the cheerful flickering fire, the curtains moving occasionally as the cold winter air from outside intruded through the ill-fitting windowpanes, Nora turned to Maggie and asked, 'Maggie....' She stopped.

Her niece looked at her enquiringly.

'Maggie...' Nora began again.

'What is it, Auntie Nora?'

'I've got something to tell you that might help you feel better in your situation. It's about something that happened to me during the war. I'm not proud of it, Maggie. But, I can't say that I feel guilty, either. Sad, more than anything.'

Maggie stopped knitting and rested the tiny, almost finished, white garment on her knee. She looked at her aunt, waiting for her to carry on.

Nora's gaze turned back to the hot burning coals in the grate and paused before she continued. 'During the war, whilst Billy was away on active service, I met an American soldier. There were a lot of them in Hull at that time. I was serving behind the bar at a dance hall. Lance, he was called. He was so handsome, Maggie, I fell in love with him the first time I saw him. I couldn't help myself. He had such wonderful blue eyes. He had a way of looking at you that made you feel special, that you were important to him. He told me he loved me and I believed him. When I became pregnant, he told me he was thrilled and that he would marry me. Just after that, I learned he had been sent to Norfolk. I waited for him to get in touch with me but he never did. I think he had known he was leaving Hull and would not be coming back. He used me, Maggie.' Nora's eyes were still focused on the glowing embers in the grate. She wiped away a few stray tears from her cheeks. 'I still try not to hate him.'

'I'm so sorry, Auntie Nora. It must have been terrible for you,' Maggie said gently.

Nora looked at her. 'At least you know that Andy really did love you, Maggie. I was obviously an easy catch. Your mam called me cheap. But, I knew that she felt sorry for Billy. She helped me a lot, though.' Nora shrugged her shoulders and gave a sardonic smile She has never let me forget what she did for me.'

Maggie realised that the pieces missing from an unfinished jigsaw belonging to the past, Nora's past, were beginning to fall into place. The constant innuendoes, unanswered questions, could now be brought out into the open. And Maggie felt her aunt's deep sorrow. She understood the open wound that could never be healed. She reached out and touched Nora's hand, they wept together.

'Did Uncle Billy find out about the baby?' Maggie asked quietly, returning to her knitting, trying not to break the spell between them.

'No, he never came back from the war. The gossips didn't get the chance to tell him,' Nora replied, wryly. 'It didn't really matter. They couldn't have proved anything. And, in any case, it wasn't their business although they tried to make it so.'

'What happened to the baby?'

'That's another story,' her aunt replied. 'It can wait until another day. It's you who's important now. And my great niece or nephew.'

Although Maggie was impatient to hear the rest, she did not encourage Nora to reveal anything more.

'You've not long to go, now, Maggie. Have you decided what you are going to do?' Nora looked at her niece, questioningly. Receiving no answer, she continued. 'I'll be here for you, Maggie, when your time comes, I promise, so don't you fret. As soon as the pains start, you must let me know straight away, even if it's in the middle of the night. It happens that way sometimes. But now let's have a cup of tea.'

Maggie put her knitting down and prepared to stand up. But Nora gently pressed on her niece's shoulder, forcing her to remain in her seat.

'You sit there, love. I'll make it.' Nora walked towards the kitchen door.

Maggie stared into the fire. The warm glow from the embers was slowly disappearing; like time itself.

Andrew Paul arrived in the world two weeks early, exercising his lungs and limbs to full advantage. His head was encased in a gossamer veil. The midwife was going to take it away, Maggie insisted that it be left in the room; there were many people within the fishing community who would pay a high price for a caul; it was believed to have magical powers. *'Those who are born with one will never drown.'* Maggie had no intention of ever parting with it. Apart from its significance, it would always be a tangible reminder of her son's birth. Only the midwife, Nora and herself knew of the caul's existence.

'You've got a lot of fighting to do, little boy,' Maggie told her new son. She was weeping as she held him tightly. 'I'll always love you and hope that, one day, I shall be able to tell you that again.'

'He's going to grow up to be a wonderful man, Maggie,' her aunt whispered. 'The caul around his head was a good sign. He will have a safe and happy life.'

Chapter 4

It was Maggie's first day back from Beverley and she had no intention of satisfying a nosey neighbour's appetite for gossip; especially that of Mrs Adamson, whose vicious tongue could make a saint sound like the devil. But Maggie had been unable to avoid her; they had met face-to-face as she turned the corner of Victoria Street on her way home from the bus station.

'Hello, Maggie, it's nice to see you back. How's Nora?'

'She's fine, thanks, Mrs Adamson,' Maggie replied, without stopping. 'I'll tell her you asked after her, the next time I see her '

'Yes, do that, Maggie,' said Mrs Adamson. 'You're looking none so good yourself, lass,' she added.

'I'm fine,' Maggie said over her shoulder. 'Nosey old bag', she added under her breath.

Maggie knew she had lost a lot of weight. Dark circles outlined her dull green, sunken eyes. She felt she would never laugh again; it was much easier to cry. She would have to return to work soon; her mother could not afford to keep her for nothing. Besides, it would stop her from thinking too much.

She approached the familiar doorstep and hesitated, nervously; would her mother be pleased she was home? She hoped that John would be in. Martha had rung Nora a couple of days ago and mentioned that he was expected to be home from sea the day before Maggie's return. John and Maggie had not seen each other since before she went away.

As she walked through the door into the living-room-cum-kitchen, she saw John seated at the table eating his dinner. He looked up and beamed at his sister. Then his face changed; he looked shocked. The last few months had not dealt kindly with Maggie and it showed.

'Do you want a cup of tea, Maggie? There's one in the pot,' John asked her, taking the old, dilapidated suitcase from her and putting it near the door. It had travelled thousands of miles before its recent journey to Beverley. Terry had used it during the war.

Maggie looked at her brother, gratefully. 'I'd love a cup, please John,' she answered. 'Where's mam?'

'She's in Mrs Lovett's. Giving her a bit of dinner.'

'Some things never change,' Maggie pointed out. 'She's still letting my mother run after her, the old battle-axe.'

'Yes, but she is getting on a bit,' John reminded her.

'She hasn't always been old,' Maggie pointed out. 'But, she's always been a nasty bugger.'

Mrs Lovett lived next door; a nosey, cantankerous old woman. Martha felt sorry for her. But she also resented her neighbour hammering on the wall at the least sound of raised voices; usually when Terry Bell, Martha's husband, was home.

It was hard for Maggie to believe that she had only been away for a few months. It seemed like a lifetime.

'How's Auntie Nora?' John asked her for something to say. He put a cup of tea on the table.

'She's fine,' replied Maggie, without looking at him. 'I'm glad I've seen you before you've gone back.'

'I'm sorry I didn't get to Auntie Nora's to see you, Maggie,' John told her, apologetically. 'But I don't get home for long. And, if it's weekend, there aren't many buses running.'

'It's all right, John, don't worry about it,' Maggie replied wearily. 'I know you would have come if you could.' She was not really sure if she believed that. Pat had visited her three or four times; her mother had only managed to see her twice.

'I'm going back again, tomorrow,' John said. 'But dad will be back next week. He'll be looking forward to seeing you again.'

'Is that right, John?'

He looked at her. But before he could question her, she asked him, 'Still trying to kill yourselves for the gaffers?'

'They're not all bad,' John pointed out.

Maggie looked at him with disbelief. 'There's not many that aren't,' she retorted. She suddenly felt overwhelmingly tired. 'I think I'll take my tea upstairs, John. I feel very tired but I'll be down again soon.'

John looked at her with concern. 'Are you sure you're all right, Maggie. You don't look well.'

Maggie heard the sound of her mother opening the back gate. It gave her an excuse to evade answering him; but she was grateful for his concern. She stood up and walked across to the door leading to the stairs. Hopefully, she would be left in peace in her bedroom for a little while.

It was now the middle of July, the days long and warm; Maggie felt only the cold chill and darkness of winter. She took off her shoes and lay under the patchwork quilt, wrapping herself in its familiar, comforting warmth; it had been a refuge for her from as far back as she could remember. She had missed it so much whilst she was away and had been tempted, on Martha's first visit, to ask her mother to bring it with her the next time she came. But, she had held back; she could never be sure that her mother would come again.

Maggie snuggled further down the bed. She felt desperately lonely. She missed the feel of her baby's tiny, warm body held close to her breast before quickly and cruelly being taken away from her to be adopted. She longed for the comforting warmth of Andy's arms around her, his soft, soothing voice promising so much happiness for the future. Life was not fair. Except for those at the top, it would seem. She pulled the patchwork bedspread more tightly over her head and sobbed.

She heard a gentle tapping on the door.

'Can I come in, lass?'

Maggie knew that she could not hide from her mother forever; they were living under the same roof. She was grateful that Martha had not refused to let her in; where else could she go? But, she was so consumed with bitterness towards her that it would be very hard for her to not explode when they came face to face. Martha had made no effort to see her grandson, Andrew Paul, after he was born. For a fleeting moment, Maggie felt ashamed of what she had done; she acknowledged that her mother would be angry and upset when she knew that her daughter was pregnant, it was natural. Those thoughts were quickly overtaken by anger; her mother should have been there for her over the past months.

The bedroom door opened. Martha entered the room; tall, her heavy drooping breasts mainly hidden under an apron. Maggie could not bring herself to look at her mother. She stayed hidden under the bed cover.

'How are you, lass?' Martha tapped Maggie's covered shoulder. 'I'm glad you're back. You must now put it all behind you, forget it ever happened and start again.'

Maggie flung back the quilt. 'How can you say that? It was your grandchild I gave away; you never came to see

him. You should have been there. He looks like our Alan.'
Maggie drew sadistic comfort from the barb, aimed directly
to where she knew it would hurt her mother most. Tears
were now streaming down her red cheeks. The full force of
her sorrow and deep anger towards her mother had finally
been released; accusations written in every volcanic watery
drop. 'I hate you,' she screamed.

'I hope you don't, Maggie,' said Martha quietly. 'It really
was for the best. And, after all, you did get yourself into the
mess,' she reminded her daughter. She turned to leave the
room. 'Do you really think I don't care about you and your
son? If you do, you're wrong; very wrong. You're my daughter
and the bairn my grandson and I love you both.' The word
love was not usually in Martha's vocabulary. She did not
show her feelings easily. 'Life does not always go the way we
want it to and we have to make the best of things.'

Maggie was too upset to notice that Martha was crying
too. She pounded her pillow angrily, then once again sought
comfort under the patchwork cover, her tears adding yet
another tale to its colourful past.

Martha made her way downstairs, wiping her eyes on
her apron. As she entered the kitchen, John looked at her,
concerned and bewildered.

'What's the matter, mam? Is there something wrong
with our Maggie? Has she got TB?' Alan's death from the
disease was never far from everyone's minds.

Martha paused. 'No, she hasn't got TB. It's nothing that
time won't heal, lad, so don't go worrying yourself about it.'
She walked towards the back door and went outside. The
bolt on the lavatory door slid across noisily; Martha was able
to weep in private.

Once again, John was left wondering. This time, he
needed to know the truth before he went away. It was hard
enough worrying about the weather to be encountered at
the fishing grounds without taking away with him an extra

burden. Little things, a word or a look between Maggie and her mother, before Maggie went away, had often puzzled him. But nobody ever told him what happened; his questions were always evaded. Not even Pat would enlighten him; she must know the truth. All Keith would say was that he was sure everything was all right with Maggie; John accepted that he knew nothing. Now that Andy was out of the picture, Keith was hoping that Maggie would take more interest in him.

There was a knock on the front door. It was Pat. 'I've come to see if Maggie's back,' she said, as John led her into the kitchen. 'And to see you, as well, of course.'

'She's in her bedroom.' John pulled Pat gently towards him and kissed her , hungrily. 'She'll be pleased to see you, Pat. I know I am.' His face became serious 'Are you going to tell her our news?'

'I don't know, John. Perhaps, we should wait a while. She is still very upset over Andy. Don't forget, they had planned to get married. Besides, she only came back today.'

'I suppose you are right.'

Pat and John were inseparable nowadays, whenever he came home from sea. Their relationship had flourished soon after Maggie had gone to Nora's. There had always been an attraction between them. But, after Andy's death, Pat had been adamant that she would never become deeply involved with a fisherman. Besides, she wanted to have a good time before settling down. But their relationship had gradually become serious and she had confessed that she loved him.

The wives and girlfriends of trawlermen live a different life to those working on the land. Some relationships survive the long absences; some meander along, but a lot filter away altogether. The womenfolk have to be strong; a breed on their own.

Pat tapped on Maggie's bedroom door.

'It's me, Maggie. Can I come in?' She opened the door and walked in. 'I am really pleased to have you back,' she said.

Maggie was still lying under the bed cover. She sat up and wiped her red, swollen eyes on its myriad of coloured patches. 'Sorry, I look a mess, Pat.'

'Don't be sorry, Maggie. I'm your friend, or have you forgotten?' She was smiling. 'In any case, don't worry about it. I've seen you cry before.'

Maggie smiled back, gratefully. She was always pleased to see Pat.

'I'm sorry I only saw you three times, Maggie, whilst you were away. I wish I could have seen you more,' Pat said. 'But I work Saturday mornings and there aren't a lot of buses to Beverley on a Sunday.'

'That's okay, Pat,' Maggie assured her. 'You came and that's what matters. I only saw my mam twice.'

'You still haven't told John why you went away, have you, Maggie?'

'No, I haven't. You haven't told Keith, have you?'

'Of course, not,' Pat looked hurt. 'You know I wouldn't do that without asking you.'

'Sorry,' Maggie reassured her, quickly. 'But, I only want you, my mam and Auntie Nora to know.' She hesitated. 'I'm frightened of what John will think of me if I tell him,' she admitted.

'He'll only want what is best for you, Maggie. I know he will. But, it has to be your decision whether or not you tell him.'

The two girls sat together for over an hour. Pat sat patiently listening to Maggie talk about the baby and Andy; she did not interrupt her unless it was to ask something. Her news could wait; she was short of time. It was now four o'clock and she had to go home, have her tea and change her dress before going out for the evening. 'I shall have to leave you now, Maggie. John's taking me to the pictures. But I'll try to see you again tomorrow,' She stood up. 'I really do think you should tell him. I know he will understand and support you.'

Once again, alone with her thoughts and aching heart, Maggie sat up on the bed mulling over her friend's words. She also pondered her future. It was easier for her to accept that Andy had gone forever, than to live knowing that somewhere, not far away, someone else was looking after her son. The couple that had adopted Andrew Paul had agreed to Maggie's request that he retain his birth name. In return, she had promised never to try to find him.

———————

Terry wiped the sweat from his forehead with a piece of oily rag, which he had pushed into his overall pocket earlier that day. The intense heat in the engine room was both draining and overpowering. The tremendous hammering from the engines, as they struggled to keep the small trawler stable, made talking impossible; that suited Terry. He preferred to keep his own council and concentrate on the work in hand, using sign language when necessary to communicate with Laurie Thompson, the fireman working alongside him.

The skipper had now given orders from the bridge to clew up. The next haul would be the last; it was time to go home and the crew were relieved. Terry, a practising atheist, said quietly, 'Thank God'. His mouth was swollen and throbbing.

Fish was piled high on the deck, reaching up to the tops of the bulwarks. It had been accumulated in heaps like funeral pyres down the port side and along to the galley, waiting to be gutted. The seagulls had been well fed but it would soon be time for them to move on to other available food tables. Over fifteen hundred kits of fish already lay stacked in neat rows in the fish room, packed in ice. Financially, the trip was looking good. Until the decks were clear, and because there was a fresh south-westerly breeze blowing, the engines had been set at half-speed, travelling at eight knots.

A flying boot belonging to a luckless airman, its owner's leg still sleeping inside, had surfaced on the deck when the cod-end was released; the boot had been tossed back into the icy waters from whence it came. 'Some poor bastard will have been looking for that.' The deckhand's joke had passed unheeded, lost in the freezing Arctic wind. It would not have been said without sympathy; but not with shock, either. Human body parts often appeared on the deck, amongst the flailing fish, when the cod-ends were opened.

Whilst the ship was on the fish, word had reached the crew that the mate on one of the trawlers fishing in the same area as them had been killed. He had been trying to release the aft trawl door whilst the gear was being hauled. A mountainous wave had crashed down upon the door, freeing it. The man's head had been crushed to a pulp. He was twenty-five years' old with a young son and daughter. But, he was not from Hull. Nobody had known him. It was a bloody shame, of course, but it would soon be history. Not something to be dwelt upon; like the airman's flying boot.

All the crew aboard the *Lady Alice* were eagerly looking forward to spending seventy-two hours, hopefully not less, at home. They recognised that they had been lucky to be given the opportunity to sail this trip. Many ships had been laid up at the dockside back in Hull, resulting in a lot of men being out of work. The same fate could be waiting for the crew of the *St Alice*. The trawler owners had repeatedly warned everyone that times were hard. But, the men already knew that; they did not need reminding. They were classed as casual workers and as such could not rely upon a regular income. But, the trawler owners, on the other hand, would always fare better. Terry had warned Martha before he left home, that when he returned he could be out of a job.

He wiped the greasy, dirty cloth over his face, taking care not to press on the area around his mouth. His skin was ashen under the sweat and grime. Suddenly, the ship lurched violently. He fell sideways, hitting his face against a hot plate. For a fleeting moment the pain was excruciating. Then, he felt a gush of miasmic, bloodied, green pus oozing out of his mouth and down his chin. The stench was lost in the ubiquitous odours of oil, the men's sweat and gutted fish, which mingled together in the confined space of the engine room. Terry felt an enormous, unexpected feeling of relief; a lessening of the pain, which had ravaged his mouth since the skipper had practised his dental skills, or lack of them, upon his infected gum two days before. He spat into the oily rag then wiped his face with a corner of it, ignoring the putrid stain that had spread across the dirty fabric.

'You okay, mate?' shouted Laurie Thompson, his voice vying with the noise of the engines. The young fireman was sharing the watch with Terry. He pointed his finger at Terry's mouth. Terry nodded briefly then returned to what he was doing. Normally, Laurie showed no interest in the chief's general health. He had, on an odd occasion, grudgingly paid tribute to Terry's engineering ability and the fact that he was always seasick during the first two or three days at sea; a lot of fishermen were but they had to get over it otherwise they would never get a job on the trawlers. Not many people who knew Terry, on or off shore, liked him. He was known for his bad temper and impatience. He did not suffer fools gladly. But, it was acknowledged that he was an expert in the engine room.

Terry had had a rough time over the last few days but, not once, had he been heard to complain. Two strong deckhands had held him down, whilst the skipper had yanked out two teeth; one was rotten, the other had become loose during the extraction. Terry had refused a large dram of the hard stuff, which the skipper had said would anaesthetise him, knowing that it would affect his ability in the engine room. 'Right,' the skipper had said to his chief afterwards, 'You'll be okay now, mate, so let's keep you and those engines moving 'til we get home. We don't want you getting bloody bed sores, do we?' He had laughed as he handed Terry a cracked beaker filled with water. 'Rinse your mouth out with that.' Terry had muttered his thanks but declined the beaker. One of the deckhands, who had held Terry down, had passed the large dram of whisky, which Terry had earlier refused, into the skipper's outstretched hand. 'I needed that,' the skipper had said after he had gulped it down in one go. Terry had made no comment; he had not been in a fit state to do so, but his eyes had clearly shown his disgust. He had felt so grateful it was all over. It was a pity it had turned septic later. But, now that the poison had been released from his swollen gums, he hoped he would be able to concentrate on getting the ship home, without his mind being dulled by the pain; a lot of responsibility lay on his head.

Because the weather was deteriorating, and there was still a great deal of fish on deck to be gutted and stored away, the deckhands needed all the help that could be made available to them. The skipper gave them a hand, leaving the bosun to keep watch on the bridge. The engineers could not be spared. Once the decks were cleared, the order would be given to the engine room for full ahead. The sky had darkened, the clouds looked ominous and low. The wind had strengthened and the barometer had fallen. Everyone knew a severe gale was inevitable.

Like most fishermen, Terry could not swim. 'Why prolong the agony if the ship went down in the icy seas? Run on the bottom as fast as you bloody well can,' was the general advice given. 'It would be a pity, of course, if one of the owners fell into the sea,' someone had been heard to remark, sarcastically. 'But it'd be highly unlikely that they'd be surrounded by mountainous waves and bloody big lumps of floating ice. They'd be cruising around in their private sailing boat with their toffee nosed kids.'

At last, the decks of the *Lady Alice* were clear and the trawl doors and gear secured; Terry could now steam full ahead. The skipper had decided to head home in the relative safety of the Norwegian fjords. Terry had spent a lot of time in the area during the war, minesweeping, so the spectacular scenery held little allure for him. He knew that the area was notoriously hazardous for small vessels, such as trawlers; heavy snowstorms batter the coastline for many weeks of the year.

As the trawler neared Lodigen, the skipper radioed for a pilot to come aboard to assist navigation through the channels, rocks and reefs down the coast to Honingsvaag. Once the open sea was reached, the pilot was able to return to his home base, leaving the *Lady* Alice to fend for herself.

Although the wind had dropped slightly, sleep eluded most of the crew. The sea was on the beam and the ship was rolling violently, steaming at thirteen knots. Everyone was looking forward to greeting the Scottish coastline and hearing the welcoming sounds of Radio Luxemburg.

As morning broke on the final day of the trip, the crew began the task of cleaning the ship. Everywhere had to be made spick and span; the decks scrubbed, the bridge cleaned to perfection, the wheelhouse windows polished inside and out. All brass-work had to gleam, accommodation made spotless; the liver house, boilers and baskets had to be thoroughly cleansed to eliminate all traces of raw liver, blood and slime. Although, of necessity, the engineers and firemen had maintained a high standard of cleanliness and maintenance at the fishing grounds, everything in the engine room was given a final overhaul. At one o'clock, the last meal of the trip was served. Pots and pans were immaculate when they were stored away.

When Flamborough Head was at last behind them, the crew bathed and shaved, then put on their go-shore suits. They were soon making their way up the muddy Humber to Killingholme Light, to await instructions over the radio to up-anchor; Spurn Lightship was a forgotten monument. The next high tide was due in four hours. They had been allocated landing number three, following behind the *Adronicus* and the *Toledo*.

The reflections from the city lights on the river were always a welcome sight. Proof that, at last, the crew were safely home; soon they would be on dry land. But, there was still work to be done. The men had been separated into two groups. Lengths of damaged warps had to be pulled off the drums and coiled down as close as possible to the after gallows. They would be over-hauled and respliced on shore by the ships riggers. The warps had to be back on board in time for departure in seventy-two hours at the most. The work in the engine room would not be complete until the skipper signalled, finish with engines.

With two hours to spare to high water, the trawler arrived at the dockside. Manoeuvring the ship alongside the quay was a delicate operation, which allowed no room for mistakes; timing and efficiency were paramount. And, the lock pits had to be quickly cleared again for any ships leaving on the same tide.

As the ship was made fast at the quayside, two customs officers jumped on board. Trawlermen were prohibited any special allowance; this angered them. They regularly worked away from home in hazardous conditions for three weeks at a time. Didn't they deserve a reward? But, their complaints fell on deaf ears. The men were classed as casual workers with no rights.

Terry was one of the last men to leave the ship. It was the chief engineer's responsibility to back the trawler through the lock pits with the aid of a docking tug. Most of the crew had jumped off at the landing stage. The dock master's voice travelled loud and clear through the cold early morning air. 'Let go aft. Hard aport; slow astern.' The trawler was gently towed to its berth on the fish market, portside to the quay. The area was alive with activity, each man playing their part in the scheme of things: bobbers wearing clogs which hammered in haste upon the concrete, looking forward eagerly to going-home time; barrows were being propelled at amazing speeds along the dockside, the wheels rumbling loudly on the slippery ground; and, at the forefront, trawler owners and fish merchants waiting in greedy anticipation.

'Finished with engines.' Terry sighed with relief when he heard the skipper's voice. He could go home.

As he finally stepped on to the dockside, he passed Ronnie Adamson, Bessie Adamson's husband, and Mally Jordan; they were both bobbers. Ronnie was known as the weasel; he was a round-faced, sneaky looking individual, of medium height, dwarfed by his wife's tall, ample frame when they stood side by side. Like his wife, he was a notorious gossip, a troublemaker. He had been stood talking to Mally; they were preparing to move barrows laden with kits of fish to a nearby railway wagon. Terry disliked the Adamsons and always tried to avoid them, if he could. The two men on the dockside looked at each other. Terry was sure he saw a smirk pass between them.

'You okay, mate?' Ronnie enquired.

Terry hesitated. 'Aye. Are you?' he asked as he passed him by, not really interested in the man's well-being.

'Your Maggie's home, she's looking a lot thinner,' Ronnie called after him.

The two mates looked at each other and grinned.

Terry's footsteps echoed on the damp gravel beneath his shoes. His breath hung in the ubiquitous early morning mist. There was little vegetation around for the dew to cling to; a small patch of grass in a neat front garden would draw immediate attention from strangers, whatever the time of year. Many upmarket areas of the city celebrate autumn with the golden touch of chestnut trees and the fiery tones of the rowan. There were never such displays of colour to be seen around here; apart from the lights in the street at night and, perhaps, a candle in a window at Christmas.

As he neared his home, which stood at the end of the row of Victorian houses, a high wall separating the end of the terrace from neighbouring Stanton Street, Terry's pace quickened, then they ceased abruptly.

Maggie had been listening with bated breath for her father's footsteps, heralding his return home. She heard the front door opening and then closing. It was rarely locked. She had not seen her father since the night before she left home to stay with Nora. She had wondered whilst she was away whether he had made any attempt to visit her at Beverley; if so, no doubt her mother would have encouraged him not to do so. Had he missed his daughter? Perhaps, it was best that she did not know the answer to that question.

Although it was only half-past six in the morning, Maggie was fully awake. She had spent a restless night, dreading the questions she knew Terry would ask; and the answers, the lies she would have to give in return. Hopefully, over the next couple of days whilst her father was home, the news of John and Pat's engagement would detract from the reasons for her absence. Maggie decided to stay in bed until after Terry had left for the dock offices, which would be sometime after nine o'clock. Usually, he called at Rayner's pub or St Andrew's Club for a swift half-pint, after collecting any money due to him so Maggie was unlikely to see him until dinnertime.

Hopefully, the ship's voyage had made a profit, no matter how small. If the vessel landed in debt, it would show in the men's faces, including Terry's, when they returned home to their families; bad temper and depression were inevitable. There would be bond and store bills to pay, debts to clear, and the money would have to come from somewhere. Before boarding, the trawlermen always visited the ships' stores on the dock. They had to pay for everything they would need when at sea, out of their own pockets. This included their bedding and the protective clothing and boots, which were needed. Even their eating and drinking utensils had to be bought before they left the dockside. The stores were always a hive of activity when trawlers were due to leave the port; even they were owned by the Trawler Owners' Association; like the men - more profit in the owners' pockets, less in their crews' wage packets.

Maggie closed her eyes. Now that she knew her dad had arrived home, she could allow herself to drift off into a much- needed sleep; enjoy some rest until the moment came for her to face him; and his questions.

A few minutes later, she was woken up by loud voices, swearing, shouting; mainly coming from her dad. 'What's all this about our Maggie losing weight?' Terry's deep, booming voice reverberated through the house.

Maggie sat up, fully awake. She looked at the clock; ten minutes to seven.

'Keep your voice down, man.'

Terry obviously had no intention of adhering to Martha's order. 'I've had that bastard, weasel Adamson, telling me that my daughter has lost weight. I want to know why. What's going on?'

'I'm trying to tell you, if you'll just listen to me for once, and lower your voice; unless you want the whole street to hear as well as the nosey old bugger next door.' Martha was stood facing her husband across the kitchen table, waiting for him to calm down, if only for a minute. 'She's been ill but now she's better.'

'Has she had TB?'

'I think so.'

'You think so. That doesn't make bastard sense to me, woman,' Terry roared. 'Why did she have to go to your Nora's?' He paused. 'She's not been ill, at all, has she?' His eyes bored into Martha's; recognition dawning. 'She was in the club, wasn't she? Like the Gibson lass; like your bloody sister. You thought I didn't know about your precious Nora and that Yank, didn't you? Well, I bet every bugger knew. You sent our Maggie to stay with that slut, didn't you, woman?'

'You're quite right, dad, I've not been ill. I was pregnant. With Andy's baby.'

Maggie was standing in the doorway. In the heat of their argument, Terry and Martha had not noticed her there.

Terry stared at his daughter, his face a twisted picture of anger and disbelief. 'My daughter's a bloody oo'er.' He swept across the room. Maggie felt a stinging blow across her face. 'We already had one in the family, now we've got another bugger, that's as well as two in the street; the Gibson lass and the Blackburn woman. You're all the same, you bloody women.'

Maggie knew of Nellie Blackburn's reputation over the years but she had never found her to be anything other than quiet and friendly. She lived at number fourteen, round the corner of the terrace where the Bells lived, and was married to a trawlerman; her husband would surely have known if things were not as they ought to be at home. But, Nellie's next-door neighbour insisted to everyone that she regularly heard 'certain sounds' coming through the adjoining wall; in the early hours, when Nellie's husband was away. And, the gossip surrounding Ada Gibson was still an occasional talking point.

Maggie lifted her hand to her flaming cheek. She had been unable to protect herself from her father's sudden ferocious attack.. 'You're wrong dad. I've never been an oo'er and never will be,' she said quietly. Tears were streaming down her face. 'I loved Andy. We were going to be married at Christmas. Have you forgotten?' She paused, looking at him, sadly. 'I gave your grandson away, dad. Does that make you feel any better?'

Terry was silent, staring at her.

'Our Alan was born six months after you and my mam were married,' Maggie pointed out quietly. 'I can count.'

Her father turned and stormed out of the room, banging the kitchen door behind him. The house shook as he slammed the front door.

Martha looked at Maggie, sadly. 'Why did you have to say that to him, lass? What good did it do?' But she did not argue the truth behind her daughter's accusations.

'I felt I had to stand up for myself because I'm not a slut,' Maggie answered. 'And you don't have to lie to him about me, anymore, mam. He has a right to know, just as our John does.' Maggie moved towards the door leading to the stairs; she needed the sanctity and comfort of her bed and the patchwork quilt. 'I'm sorry, very sorry, that I've upset you both. But, most of all, I'm sorry I gave my baby away. I'll find somewhere else to live, as soon as I can.'

'You don't have to leave.' Terry kept his eyes averted as he spoke to Maggie later that day. 'But, I don't want the matter ever mentioning again in my house.'

Maggie noted the word 'my'. It had a lot of power and importance behind it; from her father's point of view. The trawler owners owned him. Terry owned his home. Yet, even that was not completely true. The landlord owned the bricks and mortar.

Martha had talked Terry round, after assuring him that the unhappy affair would be kept secret, strictly within the family. That included Pat because she already knew; but not Keith or their parents.

The next couple of days passed quietly. Terry spent a lot of time with his crewmates at the pub. It made life easier for everyone. He had been lucky enough to be signed on for another trip aboard the *Lady Alice,* which was due to set sail on Monday morning; early tide.

When the time came for Terry to leave, he tiptoed into Maggie's room and kissed her lightly on her forehead as she lay fast asleep. He had rarely shown her affection in that way, not even when she was a little girl. But, until now, there had never been any doubts about his feelings for her; it had shown in his eyes. He had to be aboard the *Lady Alice* earlier than the rest of the crew. The engines had to be made ready for going to sea, heading for Greenland. The ship's husband, in the meantime, would be ensuring that a full complement of crew would be onboard when they left the dockside, even if he had to rouse any of them out of their slumbers. If they were not in their own beds, he would eventually find them; invading houses, dragging the men out of their beds and warm arms without decorum. He had the law on his side.

Maggie had said her goodbyes to Terry the night before; not with a kiss, just words. The weekend had been harrowing for them all. But, at least, Terry's departure had not been heralded with words of anger. And, John would be home in a week's time.

———————

The alarm clock on the dressing table at the side of Maggie's bed rudely woke her out of a deep sleep. She opened her eyes immediately, remembering with apprehension that it was her first day back at work in the fish factory. She pushed her unruly red hair away from her eyes, which were still framed with dark circles; reminders of the turbulent and sorrowful days she had endured over the last few months. She climbed out of bed wishing she could remain forever in the warmth of its safe cocoon.

Just before eight o-clock, she walked with Pat into McKenzie's fish factory, ready to face her workmates' inevitable looks and questions; she had been away a long time. She had decided not to look for work with another company and to walk into the fish factory with her head held high; and her tongue ready to lie, if necessary. Her absence was her business and nobody else's. And, Kenneth McKenzie was quite happy for her to return there to work.

Like the rest of the women, Maggie and Pat wore white overalls, sleeves rolled up to their elbows, rubber boots and hair tucked into white turbans. One or two of the workers who knew Ada Gibson winked at each other suggestively, as Maggie walked to her place at the long table. The day passed without incident, apart from such remarks as: 'Look who's here; it was about time she got off her lazy arse and came back to work,' and 'Have you had a good holiday, Maggie, while we've been slaving away?' The women's remarks were always followed by laughter.

Whilst Maggie had been at Nora's, Pat had made a point of passing an occasional comment to the girls, to remind them that Nora was ill and Maggie had had to look after her. On the whole, the workers were a friendly bunch and Maggie was popular. Besides, the morals of some of her workmates were questionable, at the very least. Kenneth McKenzie, and his son Paul, had looked pleased to see Maggie back; Kathleen McKenzie had totally ignored her.

After a few days, Maggie felt as if she had never been away. The time passed quickly; her mind was kept fully occupied. She welcomed that. But, the work on the production line was very tiring. Her legs, feet and back, always ached at the end of the day. The concrete floor beneath her feet was as cold and hard as the slabs in a morgue and equally endearing, especially after a ten-hour shift.

In the evenings, that first week back at work, Maggie was too tired to go out with Pat. All she wanted to do was climb into bed. Sunday morning could not come quickly enough for her; she could have a lie-in. And, Saturday afternoons were always free. She was looking forward to the coming weekend; the Ice Princess was due back in Hull early on Friday morning, and John would be home.

But, late on Thursday evening the city was rocked once again by tragedy; the *Ice Princess* had been in collision with a tanker, in thick fog, off the Yorkshire coast. The trawler had not stood a chance against the might of the other vessel; and so near to home, in weather which bore little comparison to that they had left at the Arctic fishing grounds several days before.

Five men died. Their names would be posted later at the dock offices and listed in the Hull Daily Mail the following night. But, first, the trawler owners had to confirm the names of those lost to the Pastor of the Fishermen's Bethel; it was then his duty to pass on the sad news to the bereaved.

Chapter 5

Maggie stared into the full-length mirror. Her face had lost some of its haunted look. Her green eyes had learned how to laugh a little again, despite the feeling of emptiness she carried with her wherever she went. She was determined not to spoil John and Pat's wedding day by being miserable.

John very rarely spoke about the loss of five of his workmates on the *Ice Princess* last year in the North Sea. They had been so near to home. When the subject came up, John would acknowledge that he had been one of the lucky ones. He would then refuse to speak about the tragedy. He had only missed one trip in eighteen months. Again, he was lucky. Many ships had been lying idle at the dockside for most of the summer months. Things were bad; jobs were scarce. But, today was special.

Having pinched her cheeks to add a bit more colour to them, Maggie lightly traced her lips with the coral lipstick she had bought the day before. It toned in with her long pink dress, which was etched with tiny embroidered roses around the neckline. Finally, she added a touch of Californian Poppy to her wrists and behind her ears. It was a present from Pat for being her Maid of Honour. She surveyed her image in the mirror one more time.

Her breasts were not as high, or as firm, as they used to be. Fine silvery stretch marks were imprinted on the pale skin of her abdomen, even though Andrew Paul had not been a very big baby; six pounds, four ounces. Her lustrous green eyes and her thick, curly auburn hair had not changed. And she no longer looked quite so gaunt. Yes, she was still attractive; but she did not care.

'I always knew you would be my sister-in-law one day, Maggie.' Pat smiled at her friend affectionately. 'Thanks for being my Matron of Honour.'

Pat was wearing a full-length, white lace, wedding dress and white satin shoes. Her long gossamer veil was held in place by a headdress interlaced with shining beads, which radiated the colours of the rainbow. Her long dark hair hung in ringlets, framing her pretty face. Maggie had spent nearly an hour heating up the tongs in the glowing coals stacked in the grate, and carefully twisting Pat's thick hair around them. The result was well worth her efforts. Pat glowed with happiness and excitement. But, the overall look of perfection could not hide her impish personality.

'You look wonderful, Pat,' Maggie said, holding back her tears. 'I know you'll be happy with our John.'

'Our Keith....' Pat started to say.

'No, Pat, don't start that again. Not today. You know I can never love him.'

'Are you girls ready?' Freda Walker's voice echoed up the narrow, dark stairs of the Victorian house. 'The taxies are here.'

'We're coming now, mam,' Pat called to her.

Maggie gave a last glance in the mirror, adjusting her headdress of small white flowers. 'I'll see you in the Church,' she said, giving Pat a quick hug. She picked up her bouquet of pink roses, irises and gypsophila and left the room. Outside, on the landing, she wiped away a tear. Her soft, white shoes trod lightly on the canvass as she made her way down the stairs to the open front door.

During the wedding service, Maggie tried not to envy her friend; but it was hard. Her and Andy should have already been married by now but fate had dictated otherwise. The reception was held in the nearby Church Hall. Maggie stood with the wedding party at the entrance and welcomed the guests. Terry was clearly relaxed as he stood next to Pat's mother, Freda. The few tots of whisky he had downed before leaving home helped. He hated churches even more than he did hospitals; they made him feel uncomfortable. Martha always put his feelings towards the church down to guilt.

The church hall was small. Tables had been arranged in three columns with a distance of a few feet between each; one long table had been positioned horizontally across the end of the rows, nearest to the stage for the bridal party; the two-tiered wedding cake, made by Freda Walker, took pride of place in the centre of the main table; the buffet of sandwiches, sausage rolls and quiches was plentiful but simple and inviting. Everything was going as planned.

'Quiet everyone,' Keith shouted. 'It's time for the speech of the century.' He looked across at his dad, Tom. It was obvious from Keith's red face and glassy eyes that he had had a fair amount of alcohol.

Tom stood up with an almost imperceptible sway. He thanked everyone for coming; welcomed John into the family, although he had been almost an integral member of it since childhood. He complimented Pat on her choice of Matron of Honour; again, a foregone conclusion. His speech was brief and not always coherent. Everyone clapped as he sat down again next to Martha.

'Thank God that's over,' he whispered into her ear. 'I was bloody terrified, I don't mind telling you.' Like his son, he had consumed several whiskeys before leaving home for the church; it showed. Martha looked at him with disgust; as far as she was concerned, the church hall was still part of the holy enclave even though it was across the road from the church itself. It was one thing to swear in your own home and quite another to do so in God's House. Martha had noticed during the ceremony that her husband had made no contribution to the hymns or the prayers.

Keith stood up again and banged on the table. 'Be quiet everybody.'

Someone shouted, 'Are you drunk, mate? You should have been the first to make a speech.' Loud cheers followed. 'All right, all right, you lot.' Keith paused and cleared his throat. 'Unaccustomed as I am to public speaking...' he laughed, steadying himself against the table; more raucous cheers and whistles ensued. He turned to John. 'Do I have to do this, pal?'

'Of course you do,' John replied, laughing. 'It's all part of the job. So, get a move on, will you.'

'Okay, but it's your turn to get up next, mate.' Keith turned away and looked at the guests, some of whom were banging on the tables. 'If you lot will stop your hammering, I'll get started.'

'I wish you bloody well would,' Tommy Parker, one of his workmates shouted. 'I'm parched.'

'You can't be after all you've drunk,' Keith called back.

'Here, here,' shouted someone.

'It's disgusting. I don't know what the vicar's thinking,' Martha whispered to herself.

Freda Walker looked very embarrassed.

Keith finally became serious. He made due reference to his long friendship with John and thanked him for the honour of asking him to be his best man. He complimented the bridal party, thanked the caterers for the splendid buffet and the reverend for his moving service and for joining them at the reception. 'I must apologise for some of this lot, vicar,' he told him, laughingly. 'They're a common lot.' He turned to look at the guests again. 'I hope everyone remembered to put something in the collection box.' He looked meaningfully at his mates. His remark incited more booing and clapping. Keith then turned to look at Maggie, who was sitting in the chair next to him.

'Like my dad, I must also compliment Pat for her choice of Matron of Honour. 'You look beautiful, Maggie.' He raised his glass. 'To Maggie,' he said.

Maggie looked at him and smiled. She was touched. 'Thank you, Keith.'

Keith focused his attention, once again, on the sea of faces around the room. He had become serious. 'Before I sit down, I would like to take this opportunity of asking John a very personal question.' He looked at his friend. It was obvious that John had not previously been made aware of Keith's intention. 'Will you, as my best friend, return the honour to me and be my best man?'

There was a stunned silence. Keith had never breathed a word to anyone that he was going to be married. Then the room erupted with cheers and congratulations. 'Who's the unlucky bride-to-be?' someone shouted.

Keith turned to look at Maggie.

'I'm sure that most people here, certainly all my mates, know that I live in hope that, one day, Maggie, you will agree to marry me.' He grinned. 'I don't care how long I have to wait.'

Maggie's cheeks were suffused with anger and humiliation. How could he do this to her, and today, of all days. The room was, once again, filled with clapping, whistling and cheering. 'Come on, Maggie. Put the man out of his misery and say yes.'

'To Keith and Maggie,' someone else shouted. 'Let's all raise our glasses.'

Maggie stood up, her eyes blinded with tears. In her haste to leave the room, she knocked over her glass of wine, which spilt across the table, splashing the bottom layer of the wedding cake; she was too upset to notice. She would never, ever, forgive him.

Chapter 6

Brenda Dayton's piercing eyes were fixed on the sea of white turbans in front of her. She was waiting impatiently for the noisy chatter to die down. Having received little response to her rapping with the end of a large knife on the wet slab in front of her, she banged again, this time much louder. Everyone stopped what they were doing.

'Welcome back,' she said sarcastically. 'I have an important announcement to make so make sure you're all bloody listening. I have just been given some very bad news.' She paused, keeping her audience in suspense for a moment. She had a reputation as a drama queen and the role suited her well. Satisfied that she had everyone's full attention, she continued. 'Mr Paul's wife sadly passed away last night. It was very sudden.'

There was a gasp of disbelief.

'You're blood joking, surely,' someone said loudly.

'I do not joke about something as serious and upsetting as a death. Particularly when it is one of them at the top and someone so young,' Brenda replied indignantly.

'How did it happen? Was it an accident?' Pat, who was standing nearby, asked.

'No, it wasn't an accident,' replied Brenda. 'She had a bad asthma attack last night.' She paused. 'I know you will all want to join me in sending our deepest sympathy to the family. I shall also be starting a collection for flowers. You will, I'm sure, all want to give generously.' Her eyes had not left those of her white-turbaned audience. 'Now, get back to work,' she added, then walked back to her work place a few yards away.

'I wonder how much the gaffers give when any of our poor buggers join the fish at the bottom of the sea,' Clarrie Atkinson said loudly. 'Well, I'm not giving anything, sod them.'

Maggie felt a momentary flicker of agreement as she thought about Andy. Then, she considered Sara McKenzie's age. She cannot have been more than twenty-eight years' old, possibly nearer twenty-five. 'It's probably true what you say, Clarrie but I don't think we should think like that, otherwise we sink to the bosses' level.' She paused. 'I'm definitely putting something into the kitty. We don't have to give much.' Most of the other girls agreed..

Maggie had always found Paul McKenzie and his wife, Sara, to be amiable and pleasant. Paul never failed to wish the workers a good morning or good afternoon, when he walked through the fish factory to reach the yard where the lorries stood. He never spoke down to the girls or appeared superior. Maggie always felt his interest was sincere. He had kind eyes; they reminded Maggie of Andy's. Her workmates had pulled her leg about it when she mentioned it. 'Keep your eyes off him, Maggie, or you'll have the boss's wife after your arse,' Clarrie had warned her. Paul's wife, Sara, had rarely visited the plant because she had a child to look after. But, when she did, she always seemed shy, a gentle kind of person. But, everyone hated Paul's mother, Kathleen. She was regarded by all the girls as a stuck up, nasty bitch.

'Weren't any of you listening to me?' Brenda's voice rose sharply above the chatter. 'Get on with your work. Earn your wages. You can talk amongst yourselves later and discuss what has happened.'

As she placed fillets of haddock carefully in boxes on the thick wooden table in front of her, Maggie whispered to Pat, 'Paul McKenzie will have to bring the bairn up on his own, now. It won't be easy.'

'Life is never easy, Maggie,' her friend reminded her. 'At least he'll be able to do it in comfort. But, I bet his mother will interfere.'

Maggie thought of her own child, Andrew, who would be four years' old, shortly. She pushed the familiar feeling of loneliness and sadness to the back of her mind. She had done the right thing when she had given Andrew up for adoption. He now had two parents, unlike Paul McKenzie's son. She had to get on with her life and try to put the past behind her, no matter how difficult that was. Nevertheless, she would never lose hope of seeing her child again one day, if only for a brief moment.

Keith continued to pester her, refusing to accept no as an answer, when he suggested taking her out. Maggie usually found it easier to acquiesce than to argue with him. She felt constantly trapped by his possessiveness and had never forgiven him for the way he had humiliated her at John and Pat's wedding, even though it was over two years ago.

The sound of *Music While You Work* came over the tannoy. 'Come on, Maggie, let's get back to the grind.' Pat said.

Someone started whistling to the music, whilst others sang. Maggie joined in. 'Cut that out,' called Brenda. You know it's unlucky.'

Whistling could induce high winds at the fishing grounds, causing a ship to go down. It was only a superstition but few people living around the dock areas of Hessle Road would risk taking a chance with the trawlermen's lives. They did not care if there were those in the wider community who laughed at them. Those folk knew nothing about the lives of the fishing families; the tragic loss of life at the fishing grounds that left loved ones to mourn alone.

Pat bent over the wet, slippery table and picked up a fillet of haddock, which had been expertly prepared on the dock before arriving at the fish factory for packing and transportation. 'Look, Maggie. Rock Hudson's backside.' She gave the icy-cold slippery fillet a sharp slap. 'I bet he'd love that, don't you?' Giggling, she laid the fish quickly but neatly in the box in front of her.

'You had better not let our John hear you talking about smacking another bloke's arse,' Maggie said, her green eyes twinkling. Laughter and fun had been allowed into her life again.

'He'll never know, will he?' Pat challenged her friend with a smile. 'You wouldn't tell him, would you, Maggie?'

'I just might do. I'll think about it.'

Later, after finishing work for the day, the two girls walked arm-in-arm through the fish factory doors and across the yard to the gates; John was stood waiting for them, grinning.

'What are you doing here?' Pat asked him, happy to see him, but curious. She gave him a quick kiss on the lips. She had already left for work when he arrived home after docking that morning. It was unusual for him to come to meet her on his first day at home. Normally, after going down to the dock offices to settle, and having called at St Andrew's Club for a pint and a chinwag with his mates, he returned home to catch up on much needed sleep.

'You haven't been given walkabouts, have you?' Although Pat sounded as if she was joking, being out of a ship was never something to laugh about, especially when there was a child on the way. John would be sailing to Iceland on Thursday but after the baby was born he was going to spend a couple of weeks at home. Pat had started saving a few shillings a week as soon as she knew she was expecting. The baby was due in eight weeks' time. It looked, from the size of Pat's growing body, as if it was going to be a big baby.

'You'll never guess what I've come to tell you.' John deliberately paused, still grinning.

'Go on, then,' Maggie urged him. 'Don't keep us hanging on.'

'Weazel Adamson's left his wife for another woman.'

'I don't believe that,' said Pat. 'He wouldn't dare, would he, Maggie? You're kidding.'

'I'm not the one who's kidding,' John replied, giving Pat a gentle poke in the stomach. 'It's true, what I've just told you. He's gone off with Nellie Blackburn of all people. Her old man will go spare when he gets back from sea.'

Maggie thought of the scandal that had surrounded Nellie for a long time. 'People call her an oo'er but I don't believe it,' she said. 'I've always liked her. You can't ask to fall in love with someone. It just happens.'

'You're so naive Maggie, and a romantic,' said Pat. 'Just because you like her, it doesn't mean that she isn't on the game.'

'What's Mrs Adamson going to do?' Maggie asked her brother.

'All I know is that she's gone mad. Good for him, that's all I can say,' John replied. 'He should have done it a long time ago, but not with Nellie Blackburn.' He grinned at Pat. 'I'll do the same, if you turn into a nag,' he warned her. 'I'll find myself another woman.'

'Chance would be a fine thing,' said Maggie. 'Probably be an Eskimo. Being at sea most of the time, it's about the only place you'll ever find another woman.'

'I'm sure you're right, sis,' John replied laughing. He glanced again at Pat's swollen body. 'How's my son, love?' he asked her gently.

There were times when Maggie admitted to herself that she was jealous of her friend. But there was nobody else she would rather have for a sister-in-law. She was happy for them.

'Our daughter's doing just fine, thank you very much,' Pat replied, smiling. She had confided to Maggie that she hoped it would not be a boy. He might want to follow in his father's footsteps and go to sea.

'How do you know it's a girl?' John asked her.

'My mam dangled a piece of string over my stomach.'

'Well, as long as there's only one in there, love, it won't matter to me what it is,' said John.

Two weeks later, as Maggie sat eating her tea with her mother, a photograph fell off the mantelpiece and landed on the clip rug in front of the fire. They looked at each and shivered.

———————————

'Heeling over. Heeling over. Need help quick. Thrown on side.'

The voice pleaded desperately as it travelled faintly through the clingy freezing air. The skipper of the *Lady Alice* was struggling to make contact with any other ships that might be in the area. There was no radio operator on board the trawler; total responsibility for the men's and the ship's safety lay on his head; he was fighting to keep his stricken vessel afloat and knew that if help did not come quickly they were all doomed. It was an unacceptable though common situation and, as such, was the cause of a great deal of anger and accusations towards the trawler owners within the fishing community. But they did not seem to care.

The weather was appalling. Black ice had built up on the small trawler's superstructure making it top heavy. No matter how hard the men on deck tried to hack the ice away from the rails and the bridge, their oilskins giving little protection from the excessive demands of the Arctic weather, it formed again immediately. Fog had cut visibility down to almost nil. Conditions were even too bad for the skipper to contemplate abandoning ship. Time was running out; men and vessel losing a battle that was leaning greatly in favour of the ocean and the elements.

Once more, in desperation, yet with the heaviness of defeat upon his shoulders, the skipper pleaded for help. But he knew that the rest of the fishing fleet in the area were fighting the same appalling weather conditions as themselves.

'Heeling over. *Lady Alice* going down. Heeling over.' It was twenty minutes past two in the afternoon. The skipper's voice was now almost inaudible; any hope of rescue gone. 'Give everyone at home our love...' His voice finally faded into the hidden arms of the freezing hell around them.

The small trawler and her crew had been no match against the power of the sea and the horrendous Arctic conditions; twenty-two men, mostly with young families, gone forever. There was nothing left to show that the *Lady Alice* had ever existed. The greedy Arctic Ocean had won, yet again. There had been neither compassion nor pity for those left at home to grieve; the wives, mothers, sisters and lovers who had now to try to come to terms with the empty void left by the tragedy. In time, perhaps, the sea would give back a memento from what it had stolen. Perhaps many miles away from the scene a lifebelt or a name plate bearing the name *Lady Alice* would be found; a tangible reminder that the small fishing vessel really had existed and fought and lost a one-sided battle.

Members of the crew had seen three gulls on the trawler's mast the day before the ship went down; it was always a bad omen. And the photograph of Terry in his Royal Navy uniform, which had fallen off the Bell's mantelpiece the day before the tragedy, would seem to have supported that theory. Neither Maggie nor her mother had spoken a word, at the time; after all, it was only a superstition.

The *Lady Alice* was not the only trawler to be lost that day in the Arctic. Her sister ship, the *Lady Christina,* also sank with the loss of twenty-one men. Nellie Blackburn's husband had been on the ship. He had died without knowing of his wife's adultery. Both ships had belonged to Kenneth McKenzie and Son (Trawlers) Limited.

John and Pat's daughter, Katherine Elizabeth, was born prematurely, but healthy, at twenty-five minutes past two, the day after the tragedy. Although small, she had shown a noisy determination to survive. Her father had missed her birth because he was at sea; a telegram was sent to him.

Martha had brought the baby downstairs into John and Pat's living-room and was sat holding her. Seated nearby, Maggie was trying to control her emotions; she was happy for John and Pat but memories had come flooding back of another birth, a long time ago.

'If only Terry could have been with us a little bit longer, he would have seen his new granddaughter,' said Martha. She was holding back her tears as she held the baby in her arms; but that was Martha. She had lost her husband to the sea yesterday, yet nobody had seen her cry.

The child Maggie had given away seemed to have been forgotten, as if he had never existed; yet, he was really the first grandchild.

———

'There was no radio operator aboard either ship.'

Maggie's anger and frustration had erupted like a pent-up volcano spewing its boiling lava down a mountainside, intent on extracting its revenge on the world around for its own reasons. She had allowed her mother to grieve for a few days before confronting her once again with familiar insistence; she could wait no longer. If something was not done quickly to bring about changes in working practices on trawlers, another tragedy or tragedies would occur very soon. Two trawlers had gone down in less than twenty-four hours; the *Lady Alice* and the *Lady Christina*.

'Calm down, lass and listen to me.'

Maggie was so angry that she gave her mother no chance to continue. 'No, mam, you listen to me. Surely, after all that has happened, you're not still going to say it's nothing to do with the women.' Her voice rose even louder than ever. 'Can't you see that the gaffers don't care about the men? They're only interested in the fish and the money they will make from it. The pockets of people like the McKenzie's are lined with the blood and guts of our lads. I can't understand why the men are brave enough to face blizzards and icebergs but not brave enough to fight the bosses. It doesn't make sense to me.' Maggie finally stopped talking. Tears streamed down her crimson cheeks.

'We've gone through all this before, lass,' answered Martha, wearily, having finally been allowed to say something. 'Even your dad said that the trawler owners are not all bad.' Shock and grief had taken its toll of her normally smooth-skinned face. She had lost her husband to the sea and her eldest son to tuberculosis a few years ago. Her only remaining son was fishing off Greenland. There was every chance she would lose him, too.

'As far as I'm concerned,' Maggie replied, still shouting. 'the bosses are all tied with the same brush and if you're too weak to do something about it, I will.' She turned and flounced out of the room. The front door crashed behind her as she left the house. Mrs Lovett complained, as usual.

Maggie tried to calm down as she stood weeping in the corner of the small plot of land in front of the house; a sparse lawn and empty borders. The soil was too sour to encourage flowers to grow although Maggie did occasionally plant some seeds; she was not one for giving in.

John would, God willing, be home from Greenland in another week and be reunited with Pat and Katy at their home in nearby Rawcliffe Street. As Maggie started to walk up the terrace, she promised herself that she would do everything possible to enlist John's help with her campaign. The news about the loss of the *Lady Alice* and all her crew, including their dad, would have reached the *Ice Princess* soon after the tragedy. John had to be made to listen and so must Pat. They now had Katy to think about. She deserved the chance to grow up with both of her parents around to love and guide her through the ups and downs of life. Andrew Paul had a right to that, too.

Maggie attempted to dry her cheeks on the sleeve of her cardigan. She had knitted it herself in her favourite colour, blue. She never wore green; it was unlucky.

As she calmed down, she realised that she would have to rally a lot of support before any campaign could begin. Many wives with young children would be worried that their men could be put out of work if the women complained; how would they feed their children or pay the rent if there was no money coming in? They are being blackmailed by the trawler owners and somehow or other they will have to be made to realise that, Maggie told herself, bitterly. People like the McKenzie's are getting away with so much, playing with men's lives. But she was now determined that they would be forced to face up to their responsibilities. It could take a very long time for things to alter dramatically but any changes that could be made, no matter how small, would be worth the fight. Until then, more of our lads are going to die, she thought sadly.

Maggie pondered over where to begin. She knew very little about what went on aboard the trawlers. Terry had once taken her and John down into the engine room where he was working; they were not very old. It was a terrifying place; thundering engines, unbelievably hot, claustrophobic, a hellhole. Maggie had immediately rushed back up the narrow metal stairway to safety. She had never again asked to go down below; the memory would stay with her forever.

As she neared the end of the terrace, Maggie looked up and saw Keith coming towards her. There was nowhere for her to hide.

'Hi, Maggie, are you all right?'

'That's a bloody stupid question. My dad's at the bottom of the ocean, or have you forgotten?' Then she fell sobbing into his arms. 'How many more lads are going to die, Keith, before something's done about it?'

'But, there's nothing you can do, Maggie.'

'There must be. Those bastards at the top are murdering our lads.'

'If there's anything I can do to help, you only have to ask, Maggie,' Keith told her. 'I'm always here for you but you always keep your distance.'

Maggie looked at him. She knew she could never love him. He had always seemed like a brother to her; but he suffocated her. And, she had not forgotten what **h**appened at Pat and John's wedding. But she was going to need all the help she could get, if she was going to win the fight. And, she was determined to do just that, at whatever cost to herself.

———————

As the *Ice Princess* slid slowly along the landing stage in the gathering dawn light, John leapt from the ship on to the icy gravel. He did so with the expertise of an acrobat, correcting his balance as he slipped on the shiny surface of the ground beneath his feet. This last trip had been one of the worst he had ever encountered in the eight years he had been involved in deep-sea fishing.

One of the deckhands had been consumed by a towering black mamba; its long curving body, edged with a deep white frill of spray and frozen ice, had bent over the young man and devoured him as easily and quickly as any hungry reptile in an Indian swamp. The man had stood no chance against such a beast.

The pastor of the Fishermen's Bethel had already expressed his condolences to the deceased man's wife. The trawlers owners never personally passed on the bad news to relatives; that was the pastor's job. There was no doubt in everyone's mind that, along with her grief, the young man's widow would also be worrying about the monetary implications of her situation. She would probably have to find a job, as quickly as possible, to support herself and her three children, if she had not already done so. There would be little of her husband's wages due to her. The trawler owners had relinquished their responsibility from the day her husband was lost overboard. And, there was most likely a bond bill outstanding at the ships chandlers.

———————

'I know what you're saying, Maggie, and you mean well, but there's nowt anyone can do about it,' John said angrily as they faced each other across the kitchen table in his home. 'The lads can't live without money. I've got the bairn to think about now, as well as Pat. She knows the score.'

'You're just like our dad; a wet rag. Look where he ended up by giving in to the trawler owners all the time; never fighting them, letting the buggers get away with murder. They've fed him to the fishes, John.' Maggie was furious, unstoppable in her tirade. Her emerald green eyes shone like jewels, with unshed tears glistening in the sunlight that was peeping through the spotless net curtains at the window. 'We're talking about men's lives, here. If all the lads ganged together and refused to sail, the bosses would have to give in. They would be out of pocket as well as the men.'

'Aye,' John replied. 'But they can afford to be. The men with families and rent to pay can't. I'm only home for seventy-two hours, Maggie. I want to enjoy spending the time with Pat and the bairn,' John replied. His voice held a note of defeat; his hands were tied. 'They'll be back soon from Pat's mother's. I don't want you mentioning this to her, Maggie, please.'

'It's all right, John. I'm going now,' Maggie replied, not looking at him. 'Keith's picking me up from home soon. But, I'm not giving up on you. Perhaps, Keith will be able to persuade you later.' She walked towards the door, then added, 'I do understand why you are so frightened of upsetting the bosses, John, really I do. And I'm sorry I called you a wet rag. I know that's not true. But how long is it going to be before we lose you, too?'

Chapter 7

Maggie's heart was racing, her face chalky white. Keith was raging like an apoplectic bull as it struggled for its life in the arena against its tormentors.

'I've been at your beck and call for over two years; spreading the word in pubs, trying to encourage the lads to support you. I've pushed hundreds of notes through people's doors, keeping quiet about where they came from. You'd have lost your job by now if McKenzie's had known they were from you.' Maggie's arm was yanked viciously. 'Why do I get the idea that you're using me, I wonder? One minute you're encouraging me to think I've got a chance with you, the next you're avoiding me. Andy has now been gone for about seven years. It's time you forgot about him.' He tried to pull Maggie towards him. She resisted, angrily. 'Everyone thought we would have been married before now; except you, it seems.'

'It's your fault if people think that,' replied Maggie. She was trying to not let Keith see that she was shaking. 'You should never have given the impression that we would be marrying, when you gave your speech at John and Pat's wedding. I still have not forgiven you for embarrassing me. I don't love you and I wish you would accept that. I'm sorry, really I am.' She was sincere in what she said; and felt guilty for using him the way she had done. But, it was the end result that was important. Whilst she had been trying to persuade the women to fight, Keith had been encouraging the trawlermen to join her campaign. 'Try to find someone else to love, Keith, someone who can make you happy. I never can. In any case, I thought you were on my side, fighting for the lads. I must have been wrong.'

'I did it most of all for you.' The floorboards groaned beneath them as Keith turned and stormed angrily towards the door. 'I'm going to Rayner's,' he shouted over his shoulder. 'There's more for me there than there is here.'

Maggie heard the front door slam. The walls shook. 'Piss off,' she shouted to the empty room.

Over the past two years, Maggie had tried to delve into the background of the fishing industry; conditions at sea, particularly in the Arctic Circle; accidents on board ship which, perhaps, need never have happened; the loss of so many trawlers over many years which might have been averted had better security measures been taken; the part the Trade Unions play in the trawler industry; and the fact that such bodies as The Associated Fisheries, Hull Fish Merchants' Protection Association and The British Trawlers' Federation Limited had always been run and owned by the trawler owners. They still controlled everything connected with the industry, including the men themselves.

Maggie had a lot to learn but she was undaunted by the prospect. But, with the support of other women in the community, if not the men themselves, it would in the end all be worthwhile.

The results for Maggie's shorthand and typing examinations were due soon. Hopefully, she had achieved a pass mark. It had been her ambition for a long time to be a secretary but not working for trawler owners. But, jobs were not plentiful, at the moment, so she may have to take part-time work.

A few minutes after Keith left, Martha arrived home from Benson's Laundry, where she was working. As she took off her coat she asked Maggie, angrily, 'Have you and Keith been rowing again?' She had passed him in the terrace; he had ignored her. She gave Maggie no time to answer. 'I don't know why you don't agree to marry him and put him out of his misery,'

'Because nobody else will want me, that's what you're really suggesting.' Maggie snapped. 'Well, I don't care if I never get married. And, if ever I do, it won't be to Keith. Not to please you, him, nor anyone else. It certainly won't be to someone working on trawlers, either.'

'He thinks the world of you and you don't appreciate it,' Martha pointed out. 'He always has done. And, he'd make you a good husband. It might clear your head of all that nonsense about the lads at sea. It's not going to get you anywhere, so I don't know why you can't forget about it. The lads will run their own lives. They know the stakes. And, so do the women. You're wasting your time.'

'Have you forgotten that my dad died on a trawler? Perhaps, if you had pushed him he would have been prepared to fight the owners for better safety on board. Then, he wouldn't have been drowned.'

Martha's hand flashed through the air, striking Maggie's cheek with such force that her daughter lost her balance. 'You have no right to talk to me like that, my girl, or to blame me. Don't forget, you lost Andy. I could say the same about you. It's time you grew up, Miss, and saw things as they really are, not how you want them to be.'

Maggie felt deeply ashamed and guilty. Her mother had not deserved the accusation thrown at her. 'I'm sorry, mam, I know it wasn't your fault my dad died but I get so angry and frustrated. Nobody seems to want to do anything.'

'Leave it be, lass. Let the men that have gone rest in peace. Look to the future.'

'That's what I intend to do, mam. It's what I've been trying to do; look to the future.' Maggie stood up and walked towards the door, her face still smarting from the impact of her mother's powerful hand; a hand strengthened by the constant use of a scrubbing brush forced back and forth over shirt collars until all stains had vanished; Victorian hearths polished until they gleamed; doorsteps cleaned thoroughly with donkey-stone to keep up with the neighbours. 'I'm going to see Pat and Katy,' Maggie said, head held low to hide her red tear-stained cheeks.

As she left the room, its walls still holding the vibrations from the torrent of angry words and recriminations between her and her mother, Martha shook her head and sighed, deeply. 'God help her, 'cos I can't.'

———————

To give herself time to calm down, Maggie walked slowly down Rawcliffe Street until she reached Pat and John's house. She knocked at the door; as she walked in she heard her sister-in-law telling Katy that her daddy would soon be home.

Pat's pretty, impish face lit up with pleasure when she saw her sister-in-law. 'Hello, Maggie, it's good to see you. Sit yourself down.' She frowned. 'Are you OK? You look upset.'

'I'm all right,' replied Maggie. 'Had a row with my mother, that's all; another one, the usual story. She doesn't understand how strongly I feel about the lads. Nor will she accept that I won't marry Keith. I don't love him. I never will. But perhaps life would be easier all round if I did.'

'It's your life, Maggie. You must do what you want,' Pat answered. Katy climbed onto her mother's lap; Pat stroked her wavy, chestnut hair, looking at her fondly. 'But, there's nothing you can do about the lads, Maggie.' She changed the subject. 'Have your results come through, yet?'

'No. But, they should arrive some time this week. I can't wait to see how I've done. Then, I can look for a job in an office. But I won't work for a trawler owner.' Maggie bent down and gently took hold of her Goddaughter's tiny hand, admiring the length of her fingers in relation to the palms; a sign, some would say, of artistic ability. Maggie's attention turned to the child's pink cheeks and the deep luminescence in her hazel eyes, which sometimes appeared more green than brown. 'How's my favourite little girl?'

Katy beamed. The beguiling smile had been inherited from her mother; those hazel eyes passed on to her from John. Maggie watched, with fascination, the flashes of burnished red in the child's hair, which glinted provocatively as the sun's rays played with the wavy locks.

'Daddy's coming home soon, Auntie Maggie.'

'Yes, I know he is. And what will he bring home for you?'

'Chocolate,' Katy replied, with well-rehearsed confidence.

'John spoils her to death,' Pat said to Maggie, laughing. 'I sometimes think she's more important to him than I am.' A slight frown appeared on her friend's face. 'It's all right, Maggie. I'm only joking. I'm sure he loves us both the same.' She changed the subject. 'He's promised to look for a shore job when he comes home. He only went away this time to fill in for a deckhand who hadn't turned up. It will mean that I shall have to get a job braiding or go back to the fish factory, packing, to help make ends meet. Money will be short. But it will be worth it. John knows how much I worry about him when he's away.' Katy giggled as Pat tickled her ribs.

'But, you haven't done much braiding, Pat.'

'No, but I know how to do it. My mother's a good teacher. And I could work with her.' Pat paused; a big grin spread across her face and her eyes flashed mischievously. 'I could always go on the game.'

'There's easier ways of making a living,' Maggie replied, grinning. 'Besides, your customers might think they are not getting value for money.'

'Cheeky sod,' Pat laughed

'I like playing games, Auntie Maggie,' Katy said, innocently.

'Yes, I know you do, Katy,' Maggie replied. She looked at Pat, seriously once more. 'I'm sure John will find something if he tries hard. Besides, from my point of view, he'll be one less for me to worry about.' She pondered for a moment. 'But who will keep an eye on Katy if you go out to work?'

'If I'm working with my mam, I'll take Katy with me. It won't be a problem. There's a shortage of good braiders nowadays. According to my mother, the latest machines can't do as good a job as the women can. But, if I go back to the fish factory, my mam will have Katy for me whilst I'm working; she has already offered. It'll be easier when Katy starts school next year. But, first, John has to find a job.'

'Can we go to see granny today, mam?' Katy asked eagerly.

'No, not today,' Pat answered firmly.

'Would you like me to take her off your hands tomorrow?' Maggie offered. 'It'll give you chance to get your housework up to date before John comes home. Besides, I like to spend time with my Goddaughter.'

'Can I go with Auntie Maggie, mam? Please, mam. Please.'

'I don't think I have a choice in the matter, Maggie, do you?' She looked into Katy's upturned face. 'Yes, all right, love, but you must be good for Auntie Maggie.'

'Oh, I will, mam. I will.' Katy jumped off her mother's knee and started to dance around the room. 'I'm going to the park with Auntie Maggie. And, my daddy's coming home soon with lots and lots of chocolates for me.'

'Hi, Maggie.' John grinned at his sister as he walked into the kitchen-cum-living room. 'Mam not in?'

'No, she's at work.'

'In that case, how's my favourite sis?' John's honest hazel eyes looked at Maggie, enquiringly.

'I'm fine,' she replied. She rarely told him how she really felt. Fishermen had enough to worry about, with the dangers they encountered at sea. 'What about you? And, what's this about you working ashore?'

John looked at his sister, sombrely. 'Have to find something first, Maggie. I don't think Pat realises how bad things are on the docks.'

At this time of the year, onshore work was normally easy to find. Christmas was less than three weeks away. Fishermen with families liked to spend the festive season at home; if they could afford to. This left more opportunities for others who were suffering financial hardship and were prepared to face the harsh weather prevailing at the fishing grounds.

This year, many ships had been laid idle during the summer months, resulting in a dearth of jobs both at sea and on shore. Now, worried wives, struggling to make ends meet and, at the same time, buy Christmas presents for the children, nagged their husbands to find work; anything to bring in some money.

The trawler owners, themselves, continually moaned that they were struggling to make a profit; but their whinging evoked no pity from the fishing community. New, flashy cars were still a common sight in front of the trawler owners' offices during working hours. Wives and families continued to be seen dressed in fashionable clothes and stylish hats; unlike the families of the fishermen whose worn-out shoes were renovated with cardboard inner soles, their only decent clothes kept for Sundays. If and when the men went to sea, their wives pawned their suits almost as soon as the ships departed, redeeming them with the same speed within hours of the men's return. The owners of the pawnshops were like family friends. There was an eidetic respect on both sides of the counter.

'I shall have to go back just for one more trip, Maggie,' John told her, gazing at some obscure point on the rag rug in front of the hearth as she made a pot of tea. 'I won't be home for Christmas,' he continued, lamely. 'I haven't told Pat yet. She'll be furious but we can't live on fresh air. And it will definitely be my last trip. No more Christmases away from home.'

'How many times have you said that, John? I want to believe you but it's difficult. I don't blame Pat for being furious with you. So am I.'

'I know I've said it before, Maggie, but I really have had enough now. I hate being at sea, especially at this time of year, but I haven't any choice. We need the extra money with Christmas coming up soon. There are no jobs to be had on shore; not the kind of jobs I could do.' His expression changed. 'I'm buying Katy a doll's pram for Christmas and a necklace for Pat,' he said softly.

'There's other things more important than money. Katy can live without a doll's pram. She'd rather have her daddy at home for Christmas,' Maggie shouted, tearfully.

'I hear everything you're saying and understand. But, you and Pat also have to realise the position I'm in,' John said, visibly upset, also. 'But, it really will be my last trip, no matter what. I promise.'

'Are you going to try really hard to keep your promise, this time, John?' Maggie looked earnestly into her brother's eyes.

'Nobody can try harder than I do, Maggie,' he replied, looking defeated. 'I shall have to go now. Tell mam that I'll see her before I go back.'

'All right and you can let Pat know I've passed my exams.'

'You said you weren't going back again.'

'There's nothing doing on the docks.' John and Pat faced each other angrily. 'I've been asking everywhere this morning, worn my boots thin. There's no work to be had, only on trawlers. Why won't you believe me? I really have no choice but to go back to sea.'

'I don't like it when you shout at each other,' Katy said, tearfully, her bottom lip trembling. She was sitting at the table, toying with the food on her plate.

John looked from one to the other, sadly, then bent and stroked Katy's hair.

'Now look what you've done,' Pat accused him. 'You've made her cry. You've made me bloody cry, as well.' She rarely swore in front of Katy. She pushed John away as he tried to pull her towards him; she then put her arm around her daughter and kissed her forehead.

'I'm sorry, Pat' John told her, quietly.

For a moment, she ignored him, tears running down her cheeks. Then she looked at him, pleadingly. 'All right,' she said. 'One more trip then no more. Please, John. Take the job you've been promised soon at Richards' on the docks. Learn to be a fish salesman.'

'Half promised, love,' John reminded her. 'Only half promised, remember. But, I'll look for something else if it doesn't materialise.' One of the floor salesmen at Richards

Fish Merchants was leaving the company and the foreman had told John the job would be his on his return from this next, and hopefully last, trip; provided the employee did not change his mind and decide to stay with the company. John put his arms around Pat and Katy and held them tight in the gathering gloom. The ashes in the grate were dying; their rosy glow already faded.

'I'll mend the fire.' John stood up and walked across the room to pick up the coal scuttle at the side of the hearth. It was nearly empty. 'By the way, Maggie said to tell you that she has passed her exams,' he said over his shoulder, as he opened the back door to go outside.

The *St Christopher* was known to be seaworthy and reliable, had never been involved in any serious trouble in her five years at sea. Skipper Harry Newman was one of the best and most experienced men in Hull. It was John's first trip aboard the trawler. He knew Skipper Newman's reputation, everyone did, but he had never sailed under his command; unlike several other members of the *St Christopher's* crew.

The first three days outward bound were always relatively relaxed on board ship but the real work of trawling, perhaps undeniably the hardest job on earth, would begin soon enough. For the moment, at least, the men were able to play cards or read, whilst bawdy jokes sullied the air, most of which could never be shared with folks at home; but there were no delicate female ears to offend on board ship. It was doubtful whether some of their colourful words could be found in any English dictionary.

Trawling was in the men's blood. They hated the sea but, at the same time, they respected it. They knew that King Neptune could always rest assured that, should a battle be fought in the depths of winter in the Arctic waters and around the deep and dangerous fiords that abound the coastlines, the mighty owner of the ocean was too often on the winning side. Whoever dares to take on the freezing dense fog, the temperatures so low as to turn to ice the spray from the mountainous waves as they crash over fragile decks and superstructure, is a brave man, indeed.

It had taken the *St Christopher* six days to reach the Arctic fishing grounds; the weather in the area was bad and deteriorating by the hour. Ice was building up everywhere above deck and had to be constantly hacked away in an effort to prevent the ship becoming top heavy.

The thick gloves that John was wearing were almost useless against the unseen enemy; the penetrating, intense cold. It attacked his hands and fingers unmercifully. But, like the rest of the men, he worked on automatically without noticing the increasing numbness, ignoring his greater vulnerability to accidents; many a man had lost a finger, or fingers, and often even a hand, in such conditions. John's abb-wool socks, two pairs, did nothing to prevent the insidious chill invading his heavy boots. His sou'wester was pulled down to his eyes to shield his head as much as possible from the elements. His long oil frock was being dragged across and behind his body; twisting back, forth, sideways, by a force four wind which was intent on tying him in knots; and, at the same time, having its wicked way with the small trawler, which was rolling violently. There was no time for the men to think of their survival. There were other more important matters to concern them.

It was now four o'clock in the morning. All hands on deck for the dawn haul; time to shoot the trawl. It would be several days before the men could relax. Each skipper in this area of the Barent Sea would be intent on securing the biggest and best quality first catch of the day. Skipper Newman had studied his charts with a shrewd and experienced eye the day before.

Fifty-fathom cables were lowered away on the stern side of the ship. 'Sixteen.' The skipper's voice came clearly from the bridge; four hundred and sixty fathoms of warp to pay away, the depth of the first tow to be at about one hundred and twenty fathoms. Every twenty-five fathoms, the skipper acknowledged this with another shout from above. It was a very long and precarious process to secure the two trawl-warps. The ship had to be able to manoeuvre without the propeller or rudder becoming fouled with the trawl gear. With the prevailing weather conditions, the task was going to be very difficult; but Skipper Newman was confident that all would go well.

As the men struggled on deck, the sea continued to be relentlessly driven by the force of the wind, which was whipping the ocean more and more into a frenzied orchestral concerto, conducting it to that final crescendo, where only the conductor has the power to allow the music to die away. The slippery decks of the ship were inexorably swamped by huge masses of darkness from the deep hell, tipped by white lace crests which disintegrated and fell into millions of icy particles; sadistic pleasure was theirs as the men's unshaven faces and beards became ghost-like apparitions.

There was never the time, nor the inclination, when the ship was on the fish, to bathe or even wash; but no-one complained; only the occasional gulls acted as witnesses; and they were only interested in the bloodied, slimy innards discarded by the trawlermen as they gutted the fish. The ubiquitous stench overwhelmed any odours emitted from unwashed bodies as the men sat around the dinner table; and, in any case, they would all smell the same. Shaving was a luxury left until near to home.

With the experience of a man used to struggling over slippery decks in horrendous weather conditions, and fully aware of his responsibilities, the mate made his way to the back of the ship to assess the spread of the warps as they cut into the sea. Once his checks were completed, he bawled his satisfaction to the skipper, who then, with a slow double ring, gave the chief engineer his instruction to set a towing speed of about three knots.

Before fishing could at last commence, there were still many tasks to carry out; deck boards to be prepared, ropes and wires to be coiled and put into position, along with beckets, all necessary for the task of hauling and shooting the gear. Spare tools were laid ready; liver baskets and cod roe bags available close by. Sharpening steels in the fish pounds were being prepared for gutting and the fish room made ready for packing the fish in ice. The ice that had become solid earlier was cracked with axes and shovelled to the far end of the fish room. Boards had been put in place ready to receive the catch into the holds. Finally, all preparations complete, the crew were organised into watches; eighteen hours on and six off; that was the plan...

By six o'clock, the wind was blowing force five from the starboard side and pushing the gear away from the ship. White feathered spumes stretched high and outwards, bending to the mounting strength and will of an unseen force, cutting visibility to nil as the heavy dark water smashed over the decks. Every now and then, the ship came almost to a standstill, faltered, and moved on.

Like the rest of the crew, John was desperately tired but he could not afford to give in to his body's needs. He had had little sleep over the past twenty-four hours. As well as preparing for the dawn haul alongside other members of the crew, he had helped to hack away at the severe build-up of ice above deck. There would be no easing-up of the men's toil until the skipper gave the order to clew up, time to go home. The better the catch, the sooner that would happen. But, at least, John could now go down below for breakfast; first sitting.

At long last, the skipper's command to 'let go' penetrated the secretive freezing fog and the heavy spray spewing from the long, impenetrable seahorses, which cleaned every corner of the small trawler effortlessly and as perfectly as any housemaid.

An enormous bang followed the skipper's instructions. The noise reverberated throughout the ship as the two warps were released. Steam rose into the air and immediately froze in the sub zero temperature. Skipper Newman had earlier studied his charts, yet again, with a practised eye. All the contours of the seabed were marked clearly; the varying depths of the ocean measured accurately. This information was paramount in dictating his speed, one hundred and twenty fathoms and three knots, at a given time.

For over two hours, the skipper maintained this course, changing to port as the seabed fell, and to starboard when trawling. Then, at last, the engineers received their instructions to alter the ship's course slightly - a few degrees to starboard. As the skipper gave the order to let go, the towing block and warps pulled away from the side of the ship and were eventually released; soon afterwards, they were brought up to the gallows.

The wind was still gusting around force five from the starboard side and pushing the trawler out of the way of the gear. The huge trawl doors, having hung from chains, were now unclipped, thus reducing the strain on the sixty-foot cables.

At a distance of nine or ten yards away from the side of the trawler, the cod-ends rose from the dark depths and surfaced like a huge hungry whale flaunting its power against the strength of its opponent, King Neptune.

Once again, Skipper Newman knew that his instincts had not let him down. Even the horrendous weather conditions did nothing to spoil his moment of pleasure. It was obvious, from first glance, that the huge net was crammed with a bounty of writhing slippery bodies fighting to escape their fate. Two bags, at least, would be needed to haul the entire catch on-board.

The engines were set at slow to stern until the floating bulging net came alongside the vessel. The first bag was taken on board and suspended over the pounds. The mate released the cod-end, allowing the catch to spill out in a flailing mass. The fish froze almost as soon as it landed on the deck because the temperature above the sea was far lower than that below the surface. Gutting fish in hazardous conditions is always extremely difficult and dangerous; when the job is carried out with frozen hands and fingers, the risk of accidents is increased ten-fold; but it has to be done.

The cod-line was immediately retied and the net returned over the side of the ship to harvest the rest of the haul. The wind was now reaching force six. If conditions deteriorated further, the skipper would have no choice but to suspend operations, move away from his present position, and find refuge elsewhere until the weather improved. But, he was determined not to give in without a fight.

John had been sent to work below in the pounding room, which pleased him. It was safer; that was illogical. He was holding a large, gleaming cod in his right hand across his knee, belly up, and with the fingers of his left one he found the soft part under its lower jaw. The weight of the cod's body had pulled it down as he held it, lifting the gill and exposing the red membrane, which it accommodated. John used his razor-sharp gutting knife to cut above the breastbone and slid the point inside, cutting along the bone until it reached the exact spot where the breastbones met. He then proceeded to cut closely down the bone to the cod's tail with the end of the knife tilted, feeling for the fine dividing line between the bones. Carefully, he ran his knife the whole way down the belly to the anal opening, still supporting the fish and, at the same time, securely holding with his fingers the lug of meat and bone he had laid back. He was then able to extract the liver with his thumb and tossed it into the basket he shared with other members of the crew; the oil was valuable; extra money for the men. John was now able to make his last cut under the gullet and into the fibrous tube. He ripped out the gut with an experienced hand then, with finger and thumb, removed the small heart, which was hidden behind the fish's head at the right side. With his left hand, he tossed the gutted cod into the washer, which was standing several feet away, then moved on to the next frozen cod. He had learned to work quickly when gutting; he usually managed to gut seven or eight fish a minute. With experience, he hoped to be able to manage eleven or twelve in that time. He had to, otherwise he would be of no use to the rest of the men working in the pound.

With the ship rolling more and more violently and the sea intent on destruction, the skipper uttered a sigh of relief as the remainder of the catch was finally hauled over the side of the vessel. The ship's mate cut the cod-end, releasing its slippery squirming mass.

The men stared with horror at the five-foot long object resting amid the mountain of fish on the deck.

———————

'It is not unusual for skippers to go off the air for several days.' Christopher Anderson, owner and Chairman of the Anderson Group of Trawler Owners Association, spoke confidently to the reporter from the Mail. 'They know what they're doing. They're experienced men. They've probably found good fishing areas and keeping them to themselves. It's quite normal. No reason for any concern, yet.'

As he held the telephone in one hand, he lifted his brandy glass to his mouth with the other and sipped the fiery, golden liquid; it burnt the lining of his throat, in a pleasant satisfying way, as it slid warmly down to his stomach. He returned the glass to the table, placing it next to a crystal ashtray on which lay an unlit cigar. He spoke calmly and precisely. 'If we don't hear anything in the next couple of days, we'll obviously look into the situation further.'

'You are definitely not worried about the vessel, at the moment?'

'That is quite correct.'

'You'll get back to us then?'

'Of course.'

'Thank you for your time, sir.'

'Good bye.' Christopher Anderson returned the telephone to its resting place. He picked up the cigar and bit hard on the butt, expelling the end into the copper waste bucket nestling in a corner of the marble hearth. He flicked a switch at the side of the fireplace. The driveway in front of the large Georgian house was immediately wrapped in a myriad of twinkling fairy lights. A large Christmas tree had been erected, and decorated, near to the porch. Glass baubles blinked and sparkled, changing colour at random intervals; a curving stairway of pale lights along the sides of the drive gently traced its way down to the main gates of the house.

Christopher Anderson sighed, thoughtfully, as he gazed out of the lounge window. It was late afternoon. The world beyond the garden would soon be hidden from his view behind a cloak of darkness. It had started to snow. The lights from the Christmas tree turned the sparkling flakes into a pavanine display of dazzling colours, before they settled on the sparkling roof of the large saloon car in the drive.

As the trawler owner turned his back on the wintry outside world, he became conscious of the wind howling in the chimney. His eyes were drawn to the flames in the grate, as they flickered to its tune. Heavy snow was forecast for later. He shivered, briefly, in the gloom, before turning on the lights decorating the six-foot Christmas tree standing in a nearby corner of the room. Tinsel, draped around the large bevelled mirror above the fireplace, waved and twinkled almost imperceptibly, as he softly passed by. The maid had tastefully dressed the room; not too lavish, nor too sparse - enough to acknowledge the festive spirit of the occasion and to appear welcoming when guests came to the house.

As he prepared to walk towards the door, Christopher surveyed his affluent domain. He had worked hard to achieve success; with the help of family fortunes over the years. His chest swelled with pride and deep satisfaction. The room was cosy, warm and comfortable room. It held an ambience of safety and security; conveyed a feeling of homeliness and contentment. Christopher's conscience pricked him, albeit only briefly, as he remembered the men who were currently struggling in freezing, harsh conditions on his vessels in the Arctic waters.

But, the loss of a trawler did not only affect the crews and their families, it also had far reaching effects for the companies which owned the vessels. Certainly, a loss of revenue over the past year had been realised by everyone, including Christopher Anderson and his fellow directors. Profits were well down. This was, in the main, due to Iceland extending its fishing limits around the island's coastline. Ships in Hull and Grimsby had had to be laid idle during the summer months.

It is always sad when men are lost, Christopher Anderson told himself, solicitously. But the fishermen know the risks.

———————

Harry Newman's voice struggled faintly, over the airwaves. 'Need help urgently. Need help urgently. Exploded mine. Portside gone. Desperate. Can anyone hear? Anybody receiving?' He was losing blood heavily. One of his hands had been severed in the blast. His head was bleeding profusely from a deep gash.

Blizzard conditions had raged unabated for the last twenty-four hours. Visibility was down almost to nil. The swollen, angry sea played the beleaguered *St Christopher* with ease as it fought for its life. Badly injured crewmen, who had survived the blast from the mine, were treated with no compassion by the elements. They were tossed and bandied around like driftwood. Luck alone was keeping the badly holed trawler afloat, at the moment.

'I hear you. I hear you.' Albert Jenkinson's voice was a prayer answered; he was the skipper of the *Lady Marina*, which was also trawling in the same area of the Barent Sea. 'Be with you as soon as we can. Problems ourselves. Try to hold on.'

When the *Lady Marina* had taken the desperate call for help from the *St Christopher* she had, herself, been battling head-on against the very severe weather, in an effort to find a safe haven to drop anchor until the weather improved. The deckhands had been struggling since early morning to hack away the densely packed ice on the bridge and whaleback. They worked with numb hands, their thick mittens useless. They performed their tasks like robots. The mate and bosun took turns to ensure that the radio kept working.

'Still here, *St Christopher*. On our way. On our way. Any casualties?' The skipper knew that the chances of the *St Christopher*, and any remaining members of her crew, surviving in these conditions, and after taking on a mine, were slim.

'Can't... much longer.' Skipper Newman's voice was almost imperceptible now. He gave no indication as to how many survivors there might be. 'Situation getting... Need... desperately. Taking in water. Heavy... Tell those... home... love...'

Then, silence descended, leaving nothing to indicate whether Skipper Newman was still alive; nothing to confirm the fate of the *St Christopher* and its nineteen crew.

Neither the *St Christopher* nor the *Lady Marina* had had a radio operator onboard when they left Hull; but both skippers had obtained a Telephone Operator's Certificate, which qualified them to undertake such duties. Without a skipper to operate the radio, the danger to ship and crew would be increased immensely; that was the general opinion in the fishing community but the trawler owners would dispute this, totally.

The agreement for skippers to act as radio operators onboard ship had been supported, in principal, by the trade unions, some time ago. It was better to do that than have no 'sparks' at all on board. But it was a deep source of anger throughout the fishing community. The practice was deemed unsafe. As always, the bastard trawler owners are playing with the crew's lives, the fishermen argued. But, their opinions made no difference to the outcome of the situation; especially as the skippers had gone along with, and accepted, the practice, fully aware that it placed an extra responsibility upon their already heavily burdened shoulders. They were regarded on the docks to be as bad as those at the top, the money-grabbing owners. The policy worked well under normal conditions. When the trawlers were on the fish in harsh and hazardous conditions, it was a different story. The practice could mean life or death for everyone. Without a skipper or a radio operator, it was highly questionable who could take over the radio duties; probably nobody but, in any case, it could be too late.

'Calling all ships. Calling all ships...' Albert Jenkinson's voice searched for contact with any other ships in the vicinity. Nothing. Silence.

The *Lady Marina* struggled head to wind against the heavy swell of the sea, making for the area where the *St Christopher* would, hopefully, be found, still afloat; with survivors.

It took what seemed forever for the *Lady Marina* to reach the area where, hopefully, the *St Christopher* would still be afloat and waiting for help. Albert Jenkinson gave a deep sigh of relief as he caught sight of a small trawler appearing to flit in and out of the blizzard; ethereal; amorphous; tantalizing. Then he saw nothing. Perhaps, it had been a figment of his imagination, built around hope. The force of the wind had slightly abated, the swell of the sea less volatile. But, any rescue attempt would still be extremely hazardous for both vessels; if it was still afloat.

'We see you now, *St Christopher*. Can you hear us? Can you hear us?' There was no answer. 'Acknowledge if you can, *St Christopher*. Repeat, acknowledge.'

Amazingly, Harry Newman's voice came weakly, as if from the grave. 'I hear you... hear you...'

'Trying to...' Albert Jenkinson's voice trailed away; the aerial had no longer been able to withstand the heavy build-up of ice and had crashed down on to the freezing deck below. The two trawlers were now completely isolated in the harsh and bitter environment, the terrifying blackness of the Arctic hell, neither knowing if the other still existed.

The headlines in the local Mail were stark and to the point.

TWO SHIPS LOST.
THIRTY-NINE MEN DROWN.
WHY DID IT HAPPEN? FAMILIES
DESERVE TO KNOW THE TRUTH.

Six days ago, a reporter from the Mail spoke to Christopher Anderson, Chairman and director of the Anderson Group of Trawlers Association, and was assured, there 'was not as yet any cause for concern.' Yet

*nothing had been heard from either the St Christopher
or the Lady Marina, a McKenzie's vessel, for several
days...*

Maggie's eyes were resting on the doll's pram standing in
the corner of the kitchen. Was that really what it had all been
about; a present for Katy? John had paid the ultimate price
for something so trivial. One last trip, he had promised.

Maggie pondered the irony of his words, as the rays of
the winter sunlight through the window struck the deep jade
of her eyes; like emeralds touched by the light of a candle.
And her anger fired those sparks; he should not have gone.
But, her deepest anger was not aimed at John.

Christopher Anderson, and the rest of the trawler
owners, had enjoyed the luxury of a festive Christmas with
their families; safe in their heated, expensive homes, paid for
with the blood of fishermen. Young men, most of who had
left widows with young families struggling to make ends
meet. There would be no pensions for them. No savings to
fall back on.

Never had there been so much anger and bitterness felt
throughout the fishing community. Two trawlers lost at
arguably the most important time of the year for families to
be together. Tempers flared in the pubs, at street corners,
in work places. There were many questions demanding
immediate and satisfactory answers. Why, when the trawler
owners had heard nothing from either the *St Christopher*
or the *Lady Marina* for several days, weren't other vessels
in the area asked to investigate? Why did the trawlers
leave Hull without a fully qualified radio operator? The
Telephone Certificate, qualifying the skippers to take on
the responsibility was not enough. It was a tragedy waiting
to happen.

Every time Maggie thought about it, she raged inside. Before going to sleep every night, she made a solemn promise to herself: I'll fight every way I can to stop it from happening ever again, no matter how long it takes; months, years, it doesn't matter. No longer are those bastards going to be allowed to get away with murder. They are murderers of the worst sort; callous and greedy. It is all about money.'

One night, she was sure she heard John's gentle voice chiding her; you can't do anything about it, Maggie. It's the way it is.

No, John, it's the way it was.

Chapter 8

———————

Pat's face was gaunt; her eyes dull and sunken, almost lost beneath dark shadowed lids. Yet her tears were less frequent now.

As Maggie walked across the room towards the table, her clothes hanging loosely around her slender shape, Pat looked up from the book she was reading and smiled warmly; best of friends as well as sister-in- laws, always there for each other, a shoulder to cry on or an understanding, listening ear. As children, they had survived the dark days of war; when the city crouched and cried under the onslaught of the German bombs. But the years had been interlaced with laughter as well as sadness. Now, once more, they needed to draw solace from each other.

Maggie put her arms around her sister-in-law's shoulders, giving her an affectionate hug, then sat down on the nearby well-worn but comfortable settee. The springs growled.

Before they had had the chance to catch up on each other's news, they heard the front door open. It closed noisily. Keith walked into the room with Katy.

'One good girl returned to her mam,' he said, smiling at Pat.

Katy rushed across to her mother and flung her arms around her. 'Hello, love,' Pat said. 'Have you had a good time at Grandma Walker's?'

The beautiful smile on her daughter's face gave her the answer she needed.

Keith turned to Maggie. 'Are you all right?' He sat down next to her on the settee.

'Yes, thanks, what about you?'

'I'm okay,' he replied.

Maggie had appreciated his support over the last few weeks. Several times, she had cried on his shoulder, allowing him into her life without any thought of the consequences. She had been distraught and vulnerable since the loss of her remaining brother; but she never forgot that Pat was the one who was most in need of comfort. But, without realising it, Maggie had been sending out false messages to Keith; giving him hope of a future for them together.

'How's your mam?' he asked her.

'Not so good, still sitting in a chair all day, rocking back and forth, saying that John will be coming home soon, so she will have to finish the socks she has been knitting for him. Her mind's gone, Keith. But, Auntie Nora is very patient with her. I could never have managed without her help.'

'It's a shame, Maggie, but perhaps it is better that way.' Keith pointed out. 'How's work gone, today?'

'You won't have heard yet. Neither of you will,' Maggie replied, angrily. 'That bloody cow, Kathleen McKenzie, sacked me this afternoon.' She turned to look at Pat. 'That's what I came to tell you,' she said.

'What have you done?' Pat enquired. 'Or, do I really need to ask?'

Maggie noticed a genuine flicker of interest in Pat's eyes. For a moment, it surprised her, but this was immediately followed by pleasure at the renewed sign of life returning to her friend's face.

'No, I don't suppose you do.'

'Have you been causing trouble, Maggie?' Keith asked her, with the glimmer of a smile.

'I was trying to persuade the lasses to go with me to the offices to protest on behalf of the lads. Someone at the top's got to listen to us, Keith. The stuck-up cow heard me. Said she wanted to see me in the office; on my own, immediately.'

'She must have been absolutely furious,' said Pat, showing a re-awakening of her inherent sense of fun.

'Yes, she was. Her face was a picture. It was bright red. Nearly the same colour as her dyed hair,' Maggie replied. 'She looked demented. Seeing her like that was almost worth losing my job.' She grinned with satisfaction.

'She's probably never had anyone stand up to her before,' Keith pointed out. 'I'm proud of you, Maggie.'

'Was Mr McKenzie in the office when you were sacked?' asked Pat.

'No, but Paul McKenzie was. He suggested I apologise to his mother. "No bloody way," I told him. Well, not in those exact words,' Maggie admitted. 'But, it was strange. I felt sure he was trying not to smile.'

'What did the girls say, when you asked them to go to the office with you?' Pat asked.

'One or two didn't want to, at first, but I pointed out to them that the bosses wouldn't sack all of us. Who would do the work, packing their stinking fish?'

'Mrs McKenzie,' Keith suggested, with a grin.

'Seriously, Maggie, what are you going to do for money?' Pat asked her, looking concerned. 'You won't be able to go on the dole. Not if you've been sacked. And, your mam can't work. How are you going to pay the rent and the bills. What about money for food?'

'It's not going to be easy. I know that, Pat. But, I'm not giving up now; no matter how long it takes, or how hard. This is only the beginning. Tomorrow, when the lasses leave work, I'll be at the factory gates. They've got to listen to me.'

'Good for you,' said Keith. 'If I can get away from work early, I'll join you.'

'Thanks, Keith.' Maggie looked at them both. 'I did nothing today on the spur of the moment. I'd been thinking about it for quite a while. Now that I have passed my exams, I can go temping until I find a permanent job in an office.'

'It may not be that easy, Maggie. But, I hope it is, for your sake. And your mother's and Auntie Nora's,' said Pat.

'I don't think I'll have a problem,' Maggie assured her, confidently. 'But, I doubt whether I will get a reference from McKenzie's. I knew the bloody witch was waiting for a chance to get rid of me. She's never liked me and she hated to see her son talking to me. You could see it in her face. If looks could kill...' Maggie grinned. 'He always asked me how I was when he passed me in the factory. He's nice. Not at all like his mother.' She noticed that Keith's expression had changed. 'But, he's still a McKenzie. One of those bastards at the top.' She bit her bottom lip. 'Sorry, Pat, I forgot that Katy was in the room.'

'Did you say a naughty word, Auntie Maggie?'

'Yes, I did and I'm sorry, Katy. I must try not to do it again.' Maggie stood up, straightening her coat. The springs murmured with relief. 'I'll have to go now.'

'I'll walk part of the way with you, Maggie,' Keith offered.

As they left the house, Maggie linked her arm comfortably through his. He looked at her with surprise; then pleasure. Maggie's body stiffened then she released her arm and let it drop to her side.

———————

'Hello, lass.' Nora always greeted Maggie with a smile. 'How's Pat?'

'She's looking better, Auntie Nora. She even laughed today.' Before sitting down, Maggie walked across to her mother, who was sitting in exactly the same position as when Maggie had left her that morning; still rocking back and forth in a world of her own, to music that only she could hear. 'Hello, mam.' Maggie longed for the day when she would be acknowledged with a spark of recognition as to who she was. The doctor had told her not to build her hopes too high. It may never happen.

'John will be home soon. Must get his dinner ready,' Martha said in a barely audible voice, without looking up.

'Don't worry about it, mam. I'll do it,' Maggie told her gently. There was no point in trying to reason with Martha.

'You're home early, Maggie.' Nora looked at her niece curiously. 'Do you want a cup of tea?'

'Yes, please.' Maggie sat next to her aunt at the table.

'There's something troubling you, lass. What is it? What's happened?'

'I've been given the sack, Auntie Nora.'

Her aunt looked at her, shocked. 'What on earth for?'

'I organized a march on the offices. Someone has to do it. Peacefully, of course.'

'Of course,' agreed Nora, an imperceptible twinkle lighting her eyes. The look on Maggie's face told her everything she needed to know. 'It's about the lads, again, isn't it?'

Maggie looked at Nora and nodded. In a flash, the defeated look in her eyes changed to anger. 'Someone's got to make a stand, Auntie Nora. If nobody else is willing to take the bosses on, then I shall. I've lost my dad and my brother. Pat has lost a husband and Katy a daddy. And, we're only one family out of hundreds over the years who've gone through this.'

Nora said nothing for a moment but merely sat looking at her niece. Then, she took Maggie's hand in her own. 'I think you're very brave, Maggie. I'm very proud of you. And, I promise you will always have my support.' She put her arms around her and held her tightly to her chest. 'And, don't worry about your mam. I'll look after her.'

'I don't know what I would do without you, Auntie Nora.' Maggie paused. 'I'm going to sign on with a bureau tomorrow for temporary work in an office,' she said. 'I know I can't get any dole money because I was sacked but there's plenty of temporary office work available.' She crossed her fingers, surreptitiously, hoping that Nora would not notice. But her aunt was astute; it was a family joke.

'We'll manage, Maggie. Don't you worry about any thing. The cause is just and I'm on your side.' Nora patted her niece's hand.

'I think I heard our John coming in.' Maggie and Nora looked across at Martha. Her eyes were fixed on something in the distance, which may or may not be there.

In the quiet ambience of the small kitchen, Maggie sat with Nora, enjoying the closeness she always felt with her. The afternoon winter sunlight was slipping away quickly, the dusk sliding insidiously through the kitchen window. The rosy glow of the cinders in the grate was gradually fading, taking with it their warmth.

'You've been with us now for nearly two months, Auntie Nora,' Maggie said quietly, unconsciously respecting the quintessential peace in the room. 'If ever you feel that you need to go home, you must tell me. I've appreciated everything you've done for us. I couldn't have managed without you.'

'I'm in no rush to get back to my empty house, Maggie, so don't you fret,' Nora replied, warmly. 'In any case, you are like the daughter I never had. I have always envied our Martha. But, I don't suppose you ever realised that.'

Maggie had always felt a tension between Nora and Martha; she had wondered why. She could think of several reasons but it had never occurred to her to question either of them. It would have been disrespectful, having regard to her youth and their age; but, in any case, she knew that they would probably have not told her.

Nora had made Maggie so welcome when she was pregnant with Andrew Paul; it was a long time ago and, yet, it often felt like yesterday. And, it had left Maggie with one important unanswered question; perhaps this was the right moment to ask.

'Auntie Nora...' Maggie hesitated.

'What is it, lass? Is there something you want to say or, perhaps, ask me? Don't be afraid. I won't bite, you know.' She smiled gently.

Maggie looked across at her mother before continuing to speak. But, Martha's mind was still occupied in its own sad world of fantasy. Nevertheless, Maggie spoke softly. 'Do you remember when I stayed with you and you told me about your baby?'

'Yes, I do remember. And you want to ask me what happened to it.'

'You said you would tell me one day and I've always wondered,' replied Maggie, quietly. 'If you'd rather not talk about it, I don't mind. I don't want to upset you.'

'It doesn't upset me now, not like it used to. And, no, I don't mind talking to you about it. In fact, I'm pleased you have asked. I've never been able to discuss it with anyone before, not even our Martha.' Nora looked across at her sister and sighed a little before continuing. 'My baby died a few hours after she was born, Maggie. It was a little girl. She looked so beautiful, so normal. But, her heart was not properly formed. I was heart-broken.'

'I'm so sorry, Auntie Nora. I had no idea. It must have been very hard for you, having me stay in your home when I was pregnant.Nora put her hand on Maggie's arm. 'You must never feel guilty about that. I understood what you were going through and was more than happy to look after you. I was very sorry that things turned out for you the way they did.'

'It seems a long time ago now,' replied Maggie.

'How have you coped with it? I've never felt able to ask you before.'

'I have had to get on with my life. Put what happened behind me. At least my baby was healthy. But I always wonder if he is happy.'

'I'm sure he is, lass,' Nora told her, firmly. 'He was adopted by people who desperately wanted a baby. And, he was beautiful. How could anyone not love him?'

'I'll never give up hope that I shall see him again, one day,' Maggie said. 'I know that I will recognise him no matter how old he is. I feel that so strongly, Auntie Nora.' She paused. 'He was born with the mark.'

Nora nodded.

'I still have his caul in my bedroom. Every now and then I take it out of its wrapping and look at it. Would you like to see it?'

'I'd love to, Maggie.'

Nora smiled fondly at her niece's retreating figure. She looked across at Martha, who was sleeping with her head resting on her chest.

Maggie returned to the kitchen holding a small cardboard box. Across the lid, she had written **ANDREW PAUL** in large black letters. She sat down next to Nora then lifted the box lid and took out a package of white tissue paper, which she gently opened. The flimsy, gossamer caul, which had once covered the head of the baby Maggie had reluctantly handed over to strangers, was revealed in the stillness of the late winter afternoon.

Nora gave a soft gasp of astonishment. Seven years had passed since she first saw the caul, which, although very delicate and slightly shrivelled, had survived intact. 'There's many a folk who'd pay a handsome fee to own one of those, lass,' she said.

'I shall never part with it,' Maggie said, firmly. 'Well, not until I can return it to its rightful owner. He'll be seven now, Auntie Nora. I often wonder what he looks like. Whether his hair is blonde and curly like Andy's, or brown and wavy like mine.'

'Either way, he'll be very handsome, I am sure,' Nora said with confidence. 'And, if he has your green eyes, what more could you ask?'

In the quiet ambience of the room, aunt and niece sat in quiet empathy, each in their own way reflecting on the caul. It was a widely held belief within the fishing community that the gossamer membrane held magic properties, which would keep its owner safe from drowning. They were rarely sold or given away. They were priceless as far as their owners were concerned.

Maggie always felt totally at peace when she was with her aunt, a closeness she had rarely experienced with her mother. She had never doubted Martha's love for her, recognising that Martha had never found it easy to show her true feelings to anyone, not even her own family. Maggie accepted that it was an inadequacy inherent in many people; it was in their genes.

Nora looked at the clock on the mantelpiece. 'Have you seen the time, lass? Tea's going to be late tonight.' Her eyes twinkled. 'But, it was worth it, wasn't it?'

'I love you, Auntie Nora,' Maggie said softly. The last time she had confessed to feeling that way about anyone was when she was with Andy, the night before he left home to sail on the doomed trawler, the *St Helena*, more than seven years ago.

'You'd better not let our Martha hear you say that, lass,' Nora said. 'She won't like it. She'll be jealous.' She looked guilty. The words had slipped out. 'But, I doubt she'll ever know. Poor Martha.' She smiled at Maggie. 'Put that caul back in its box and let's get you fed, Maggie. If you're going to face the trawler owners, you're going to need all your strength, and more besides.'

'They don't know what's coming to them, Auntie Nora.'

———————

'Why is that lady shouting, daddy? She looks angry.'

Paul McKenzie looked down at his young son, fondly.

'She's very upset because a lot of fishermen have died.'

'How did they die?'

'Their ship sank and they all drowned.'

'Will that happen to you, daddy?' The young boy's bottom lip trembled. 'I don't want you to die.'

'Don't you fret about that. I am not going to die just yet. Hopefully, not for a long time.' Paul smiled, reassuringly, and put his arm around the boy's small shoulders. 'I don't work on the ships or go to sea,' he pointed out. 'But, everyone has to die, Kennie,' he added. 'Like your mummy.'

'Mummy has gone to live with Jesus in heaven, hasn't she, daddy?'

'Yes, she has. I showed you her bright star in the sky, don't you remember?'

'Yes, daddy, it smiled at me. Will I go to heaven, when I die?'

'I'm sure you will,' Paul answered, looking down at his son, briefly.

Kenny looked thoughtful, for a moment. 'Did the men who died work on our fishing boats, daddy?'

Paul made no reply. His mind was elsewhere, his eyes burning with unmistakeable admiration as he watched the young woman at the quayside shouting and gesticulating wildly at a departing trawler.

He recognised one or two of the group of women who were supporting her. They had worked alongside Maggie in his father's factory but had lost their jobs when they had walked out in sympathy, on learning that Maggie had been instantly dismissed. …. for encouraging and causing unrest amongst McKenzie's female workers, in McKenzie's time, on McKenzie's property… according to Kathleen McKenzie. And, without just cause or justification… Nothing that Kenneth McKenzie or his son had pointed out, in mitigation, had made any difference to Kathleen's stance as far as Maggie, or her supporters, were concerned, either that day or since.

Maggie's hair was almost hidden under a green woollen headscarf; the colour emphasised the deep lustre in her emerald eyes. Fiery sparks darted back and forth across those green orbs in the semi-darkness, fuelled by passion and anger.

Dawn was leaving behind the darkness of night. Dim lights could be seen, travelling from a line of moving trawlers, and lonely lights flickered dimly across the quayside. A bitterly cold, north-easterly wind was beating against Maggie's cheeks, relentlessly, causing tears to run freely down her face. It pulled at the hem of her black woollen coat, which hung slightly below the cuff of the brown padded boots that she was wearing for protection against the wintry early morning weather.

It had started to snow. Unless the temperature rose, it would lay without melting on the icy concrete. Walking along the quayside was extremely dangerous. But, the group of shouting women were undeterred in their efforts to draw a semblance of support from the departing trawlermen.

They were waving their arms wildly, demanding the crew's attention.

The *St Maria*, sister-ship to the ill-fated *St Christopher*, was moving slowly along the quayside towards the lock gates on the first lap of its three week journey to the Arctic fishing grounds.

'Can't hear you, love,' one of the deckhands shouted, laughing, cocking his ear to one side like a puppet.

Maggie's angry voice retaliated through the icy air. 'We can't go it alone, lads. We need your support. We're fighting for you.'

But, the smiling fishermen appeared unmoved by her words, or those of her supporters. 'You're wasting your time, lasses,' one of the older men at the rail called down to them. 'Leave it to the lads. Get back to your bairns and your kitchen sink.'

'We've already left it to the lads and where did it get 'em? Nowhere. They didn't have the bloody guts to stand up to the gaffers,' Maggie shouted after the trawler, unsure whether her words would reach the men. 'Leave it to the lasses, you stupid, sods. We'll get something done, you'll see.'

The *St Maria* continued to slowly wend its way forward in the semi-darkness. Broody, hanging clouds barely visible as they hovered menacingly above the Humber, teasingly held back the heavy snow, which the forecasters had promised was on its way. The thick black smoke from the trawler's funnel was slowly disappearing into the ubiquitous early morning air, leaving the city behind to a far kinder fate than awaited the fishermen at the Arctic fishing grounds.

As the next trawler in the line continued to move along out of earshot, one of the women called after it. 'We'll see you later, if you get back. But, don't rely on it, you silly buggers.'

The shouts and recriminations from the crusading women continued to follow each departing vessel but were quickly lost on the wind. The black trail of smoke emitted from the trawlers' funnels, each marked with the trawler owner's crests, would soon be but a memory to the angry crowd on the quayside; particularly, if the men did not return, God forbid. They were set on a journey to another world, one with no equal; a dark, frightening environment, the crew's only friends the hungry seagulls, their enemies a frenzied ocean inhabited by towering pillars of ice, and elements which would never be encountered at home. Few miners in the company of fishermen would dare to argue that deep-sea fishing in the depths of winter is far more dangerous than working in the pits.

'Daddy. Daddy. You haven't answered me.' The boy tugged at Paul's arm, as they stood on the freezing quayside; he was still waiting for an answer from his father as to whether the dead men had died on McKenzie's trawlers.

Paul glanced down, briefly, at his son.

'I'm sorry, Kenny. What did you want to know?' His eyes immediately darted back to the group of angry women, who were now preparing to leave the quayside.

'Did any of those men die on our ships, daddy?'

'Yes, I am afraid they did,' his father replied, his attention still mainly focused on Maggie.

'Why didn't you or granddad save them?' Kenny asked him, accusingly.

Paul looked down at him, thoughtfully, at last giving the young boy his full attention. 'It was never as simple as that, Kenny,' he answered, quietly. 'When we get home, I'll explain things to you.'

Five trawlers had left the fish dock that morning; each destined to be heckled and boo'ed by the crowd of angry women. It was now nearly nine o'clock. It should have been full daylight but visibility was deteriorating rapidly. The soft mantle of falling snow was gradually being whipped into a pavanine display by the increasing strength of the north-easterly wind, which was blowing from the Russian Steppes.

Paul McKenzie shivered. He took hold of his son's arm and steered him towards the car standing nearby; it was gradually being wrapped in a soft white mantel as the falling snow gained momentum. The handsome young man turned, briefly, in Maggie's direction. She was walking towards him with two of the women who had been dismissed by McKenzie's; their heads were bowed against the swirling white flakes.

For a brief moment, Maggie lifted her head; through the white winter curtain and their eyes locked. She felt an overwhelming alien force sweep over her; it was something she could neither recognise nor comprehend. Time had stood still for her; an invisible arrow had reached the core of her being; her legs felt unbelievably weak; her body no longer under her control.

It was all over in a flash, perhaps a figment of her imagination. She watched Paul McKenzie turn quickly away and help his young son into the car. She had been catapulted back into the real world, one that was all too familiar to her; an environment where there was only 'them and us', the hated and the used. The moment had left her feeling totally drained.

Maggie thought of the comfortable, warm and safe world to which he and his son would return. The young boy would grow up cosseted in luxurious and comfortable surroundings. He was not given away to strangers at birth because his father had died at sea before he and his mother could marry; drowned on one of the McKenzie's trawlers. Maggie held no feelings of hate against the boy, only the greedy trawler owners.

One of the women walked into the back of Maggie's stationary figure, causing her to stumble slightly. 'Sorry, Maggie,' she said. Then, puzzled by the strange look on Maggie's face, asked her, 'Are you okay?'

'I'm fine, thanks,' Maggie replied, forcing a smile as she made an effort to regain her composure. 'I think the cold air's getting to me. Let's all go home. We've done enough, today.'

———————

'Are you warm enough, Kenny?' Paul McKenzie asked his son as they travelled slowly along the road away from the quayside. 'You are very quiet.'

Kenny had taken an avid interest in the various activities in which the company was involved, since he was about three years' old. He loved to go down to the quayside to watch the trawlers departing, even in the depth of winter, having his father point out to him all the different parts of the vessels. He digested the information like someone born with the sea in his veins, his interest far more acute than would be expected for a boy of such tender years.

'The fishermen are very brave, aren't they, daddy?'

'Yes, they are. Very brave,' Paul answered.

'Why were you watching that lady, daddy?'

'I was watching all the ladies, Kenny, not just one. Some of them worked in our factory.'

'Why don't they work there now?'

'Grandma said they were causing trouble and had to leave,' his father replied.

Kenny looked thoughtful for a moment. 'Grandma doesn't like me very much, daddy,' he said.

'Of course she likes you, Kenny. In fact, I know that she loves you very much,' his father reassured him, surprised at the young boy's revelation. 'I never want to hear you say that again or I'll be very angry with you.'

Kenny's bottom lip trembled. Paul took his hand off the wheel and patted his son's knee, still keeping his eyes on the road ahead. 'It's fish pie for supper, tonight. Your favourite.'

––––––––––––

'Leave me alone, you mucky bugger,' Maggie shouted, hoping that other members of staff in the adjacent offices could hear. She had returned after her lunch- break to once again be pounced upon by the owner and Chairman of Shuttleworth's Fences and Doors Limited. Sammy Shuttleworth had been skulking behind the door waiting for Maggie to enter the office.

He was a squat, obnoxious, sixty-four years' old widower, who slobbered lasciviously every time he saw a member of the opposite sex, irrespective of their charms, or lack of them. His hands were never in his pockets; it would be better for every woman's sake, if they were. He trespassed on any part of an unsuspecting female's anatomy, should they come within reach of his groping fingers. He was hated, not least by Maggie. But, unfortunately, he also paid the office girls' wages.

Jobs were not plentiful, even for those most qualified in secretarial or bookkeeping skills. Maggie was employed on a temporary basis; her second secretarial job since leaving McKenzie's. She was free to leave, in principle, whenever she wanted but financial restraints dictated that she stay at Shuttleworth's.

'You're not being very wise, Miss Bell,' her employer threatened her, his thick bottom lip drooling with desire. 'But, I'm going to forget what you said.' He grinned lustfully at her, undeterred by her rejection of his advances. 'I can help you get on in the world, if you are nice to me.' He leaned closer to her, his face almost touching hers. 'You have the most beautiful green eyes I have ever seen.'

Maggie was suddenly overcome by a savage wave of anger and disgust. Her blood boiled, the tips of her fingers tingled and burned. Without a second thought, she gave him a resounding slap across the face, so hard that the imprint of her hand stood out clearly on his ruddy fat cheeks. Immediately, she felt her body relax slightly. Her anger and loathing for the man had finally been appeased.

'You are a dirty old man. You're repulsive; ugly. There's no way that I'm staying here any longer to be mauled by you two or three times a day.'

Maggie noticed one or two of the older female members of staff watching them wide-eyed. Not once, in the six weeks she had worked for the company had she seen anyone stand up to the loathsome man standing in front her. He was gazing at her with disbelief, eyes and mouth wide open, his tongue hanging limply over his bottom lip.

Maggie picked up her handbag and left the office, grabbing her coat from one of the hooks in the corridor as she passed.

'You'll regret this, Miss.' Samuel Shuttleworth's voice echoed after her. 'You'll never work again.'

Maggie turned slightly and shouted over her shoulder, 'Sod off, you mucky sod. Stuff your job.' Then came the tears; warm wet drops running down her hot red cheeks; it was so unfair. Men like Sammy Shuttleworth should be castrated.

Maggie remembered the moneylender, who ran a business near to Victoria Street when she was a young girl. Every time her mother sent her to pay her loan money, usually once a week, Maggie had had to struggle with the vile man as he tried to kiss or touch her. The thought of his slobbering lips brushing across her cheeks, as she pushed him away, still remained vividly with her; he was another Sammy Shuttleworth. When she heard that he had died, the words 'oh, what a shame' did not enter her head. He would be of no loss to anyone. For one thing, he had no family.

By the time she reached the bus stop, Maggie's tears had subsided. Anger had given way to apprehension. She had been lucky after she left McKenzie's; the agency had taken her onto their books. Her first job had been at a firm of wholesale fruit merchants as a temporary secretary; it was to cover for sickness absence. She had enjoyed that job. When it came to an end, she had been sent to Shuttleworth's. It could now be her last position with the agency.

She would be out of work. She would have no income.

———————

'It is quite all right, Maggie. We've had complaints about him before. We had hoped you could handle him.'

Maggie was stunned; whilst she was being molested by Samuel Shuttleworth, the agency staff had known of his reputation.

'I don't suppose you would be prepared to give him another chance, would you, Maggie?' The smiling, beautifully groomed, Miss Jackson, looked hopefully across the almost empty desk. She must be a highly organised woman, Maggie thought, vaguely. Or, maybe, the job entailed very little paper work. 'No, I suppose not,' Miss Jackson conceded. She studied the book in front of her. 'I am afraid that we only have one other position available, at the moment, and I really don't think you would be interested in that...'

Maggie's eyes settled on a piece of bright red fingernail, which dared to clutter the top of the immaculate paper-free desk. It sullied the aura surrounding the immaculate woman.

'Are you all right, Maggie? Maggie...'

Maggie jumped. 'Oh, I'm sorry. What did you say?'

'I said that there is only one other job I can offer you, at the moment. But, perhaps, you need to take some time off work to rest. You don't look well.'

'I'm fine,' Maggie retorted.

Miss Jackson studied Maggie for a moment. 'As long as you're sure you are all right...'

'I'm perfectly sure.'

'Good.' Miss Jackson relaxed. 'As I said before, I have only one job to offer you, at the moment, and that's at McKenzie's, where you worked before. They need a temporary secretary for about three weeks.'

'There is no way I could work there again,' Maggie pointed out, angrily. 'In any case, they wouldn't want me.'

'Perhaps, they may look upon you differently, now that you no longer work in their factory.'

'There's nothing wrong with working in a factory,' Maggie retaliated. 'The girls I worked with are ordinary but honest. They will help anyone.'

'I wasn't suggesting that people who work in factories are to be looked down upon, Maggie,' Miss Jackson said quickly. 'I simply meant that, because you now work in an office, the McKenzies may be prepared to accept you in that capacity, on a temporary basis. I wouldn't have asked you but we have nobody else available, at the moment, who is suitable.'

'I don't know whether I can bring myself to work for them again, even if they do agree to take me on, which I doubt. Kathleen McKenzie, certainly, won't want me on the premises.'

'Mrs McKenzie is ill, at the moment, I understand. You would be working for Mr McKenzie, starting next Monday. Think about it, Maggie, and let me know tomorrow whether or not you want to accept the position; that is if Mr McKenzie is agreeable, of course.'

Maggie was quiet for a moment. 'Yes, all right but I am not promising anything.'

'Don't forget that, at the moment, it is the only work I can offer you.'

Maggie was cornered. She needed the money. And, the immaculate creature sat at the other side of the desk was fully aware of that. A sudden flutter of excitement rose in Maggie's chest. She knew that she would accept the job, given the chance. She also recognised the danger.

———————

Keith followed Maggie into the modestly furnished front room. A brown three-piece suite took up most of the interior; an ebony upright piano, complete with stool, proudly graced a corner near the north-facing window. Drab, faded brown curtains reached down below the windowsill, they matched the suite. As Keith closed the door behind him, Maggie shivered, not turning to look at him.

It was late March. The freezing days of winter had, hopefully, been left behind, but the sun's rays rarely ventured into this room, even in the summer.

When Maggie had let Keith into the house, she knew from the look on his face that he had heard the news from Pat. Martha was asleep in her armchair in the kitchen. If Keith started to shout, her mother would wake up, afraid.

'What the hell were you thinking about, after the way they treated you?' Keith's face was contorted with rage.

Maggie knew that his anger had little to do with the way McKenzie's had dismissed her. 'Keep your voice down. My mother's asleep. And Auntie Nora will be in soon.'

Keith appeared not to have heard what she said. 'What on earth's got into you? You're a bloody fool.'

'If you don't stop shouting, you can get out,' Maggie snapped.

'I can't believe you are going back there after the way they treated you. Where's your pride?'

'It has nothing to do with pride,' Maggie retorted. 'I need the money. Besides, Keith, think about it. Don't just go off the deep end and see things the way you want to see them. I'll get the chance to glean information about what goes on at the top.'

Keith stood looking at Maggie, his eyes boring into hers. She noticed that his fists were clenched in front of him. He had never before struck her. But, neither had she ever seen him look so wild, so violent. She took a small step backwards.

'I have agreed to do the job, and that's that,' she said, with an almost imperceptible tremor in her voice. 'It's only for three weeks.' Her voice rose. 'In any case, it has nothing to do with you, or anyone else for that matter, what I do with my life.'

'You must be bloody balmy.' Keith's eyes were blazing. 'Perhaps, you have an ulterior motive that you're not telling me. I'm not bloody daft.'

Maggie floundered. 'I don't know what you mean.'

'Come off it. You'll be working for Paul McKenzie, won't you? That's what all this is about.'

'I might be working for him, yes, but I doubt it. But, I'm definitely not interested in him, or any other man, either,' Maggie retorted, trying not to betray the undeniable conflict within her. The memory of seeing Paul McKenzie watching her on the quayside was never far away. 'I shall have a job to do and I shall do it to the best of my ability. And, as I said before, I need the money.'

'You could marry me and then you wouldn't need to work. Well, not full-time.'

'We've gone through all this before, Keith. I do not love you. I will not marry you. We can only be friends,

although, the way you are going, we won't even be that soon.'
Sometimes she wished he was out of her life.

Since entering the room, neither of them had made any
attempt to sit down. Keith turned and strode angrily towards
the door. 'I'm not staying here any longer to listen to a load of
bullshit. You must think I've fallen off a Christmas tree. I'm
going down to the pub. I might see you later but don't bank
on it.' He left the room, slamming the door behind him.

'Maggie, someone shouted at me.' Martha was crying
and trying to lift herself out of her chair.

'It's all right, mam. It was Keith. He wasn't shouting at
you. He's gone now.'

———————

As Maggie had walked across the factory yard towards
the offices of McKenzie's, just before eight-thirty on the
following Monday, her stomach was churning. I don't think
I am going to be able to do this, she told herself.

She received a mixed reception from the girls she had
worked alongside in the factory, as she passed them. One or
two had smirked then looked away, knowingly; others had
either given her a friendly wave or totally ignored her.

Maggie had always wondered what it would be like on
the other side of the fence; the dividing line between the
factory floor and the office, the upstairs and the downstairs.
Now she was going to find out.

Paul McKenzie was waiting for her in his office. He
welcomed her warmly, shaking her hand and smiling. Once
again, time stood still for her. Her body seemed to be no
longer under her control. She was angry with herself for
being so stupid. He was simply being friendly; a courtesy
that was normal for his class.

'Hello, Maggie, thank you for agreeing to come; it must
have been a very hard decision for you. We are desperately in

need of some help, at the moment.' Paul smiled at her, still gripping her hand. 'Maggie...?'

'Oh, I'm sorry. I feel a bit nervous, at the moment, but I'll soon settle down.' She tried to look confident. If she was to make a success of this job, even though it was only a temporary one, she knew that a professional approach was essential. Her secretarial skills were never in doubt.

'The agency had nothing else to offer me,' she answered, sharply, the memory of her dismissal from McKenzie's still being fresh in her mind. 'I needed the money.'

She saw Paul flinch slightly and immediately felt guilty. He and his father had tried, unsuccessfully, to make Kathleen McKenzie reverse her decision. It was a point in their favour. 'I was surprised that you agreed to take me on,' she pointed out in a conciliatory tone, to decrease the tension between them.

'We are desperate for help so, when the Bureau rang and asked if we would take you on, I was very pleased to say 'yes.' Paul had spoken quietly. 'I admired the way you stood up to my mother, Maggie. Very rarely does anyone dare do that. If it makes you feel any better, my father and I did not agree with her.' He paused, smiling. 'But, don't tell her that, will you?'

Maggie looked at him, surprised. 'No, I won't,' she answered. 'But, she got her own way.' Maggie felt an embarrassed flush rise in her cheeks; her large green eyes widened with dismay; she had been insolent. He had not deserved it. 'I'm sorry. I should not have said that.' She turned to leave the room, resisting the temptation to point out that it was true.

'Where are you going?' Paul looked dismayed.

'Home. I don't think this is going to work.'

'That's ridiculous, Maggie. You haven't given it a chance. I had the impression you were a fighter. Perhaps, I was wrong. But, if it helps at all, my mother is not well, at the moment, and does not come into the office. I'm in charge. And, as there's a lot of work needing to be done, how about getting started?' Paul's eyes twinkled, mischievously.

Maggie looked at him, for a moment, recognising the challenge. She had known that she would not resist; her instincts had told her that he was confident of that, also, and it irritated her. She surveyed the small office; there was a desk, a telephone and a chair. An old filing cabinet stood in the corner of the room, with an adjacent bookshelf. 'Will this be my office?'

'Yes. I'm next door. My father rarely comes in, at the moment. When he does, he will be working in his office further down the corridor. He has his own secretary. Mrs Moverley.' Paul smiled. 'If you are worried about anything, Maggie, don't be afraid to ask me. I'll leave you now to settle in and see you again in about half an hour.'

Maggie felt the familiar excitement rise in her chest; but, she also recognised the threat that encompassed it.

'What is that creature doing in my office?'

Kathleen McKenzie's voice penetrated through the wall, which separated Maggie's office from Paul's. The moment Maggie had dreaded so much had finally arrived. She would be told, in no uncertain terms, to leave the company immediately. She had a feeling of *déjà vu*.

She had been working for McKenzie's for almost six weeks; longer than her original assignment. Kathleen McKenzie had been diagnosed with pleurisy at the beginning of February and recuperation had been slow. But, she was now determined to pick up where she left off.

Whilst she had been working so close to Paul, Maggie had not been able to ignore the intangible pull, the magnetism, which she felt was undeniably there between them. She had argued with herself but no matter how much she tried to understand the confusion within herself, answers always eluded her. Familiar feelings which had been dead for so long, and which she had believed she would never experience again, had intruded into her life once more. She was still a young woman. She had needs. For so long, they had neither been recognised nor tested.

Her conscience tore her apart during the long, lonely nights. As her tortured body tossed and turned, she longed to feel warm hands caressing her body. Paul McKenzie had taken over her soul and part of her hated him for it. And, she had no way of knowing how he felt about her. But, she had to put him out of her mind.

Not once during her conversations with Paul over the preceding weeks had Maggie brought up the subject of McKenzie's trawling fleet and the men's safety. She now had to return to the real world outside, one that did not rely on the blood of men for its comfortable existence. She would forget Paul McKenzie, given time; and that was a commodity she would have plenty of if she did not find another job quickly.

Maggie knew that Kathleen had become aware of the attraction between her son and 'that factory girl' many months ago. Perhaps, even earlier than Maggie had realised. But, mothers usually want what they feel is best for their sons. Kathleen was no different in that respect. There was too much of a social gulf between her son and Maggie. Maggie understood her position. She knew that she would have felt the same about her son. But, that situation would never arise.

She stood up from the desk and made her way to the door, picking up her coat from the hanger as she passed by. Once again, she would not give Kathleen McKenzie the pleasure of sacking her.

Maggie quickened her pace, head bent low to her chest. Someone was running behind her and they were getting closer. All she wanted to do was to walk out of the gates and bury McKenzie's in the past. She would also have to forget about Paul; but she had fallen in love with him.

'Maggie, wait a minute.'

Her heart sank. She started to run.

'Stop, Maggie. I want to talk to you.' A strong hand grabbed her arm and swung her around.

'Leave me alone. Go back to your mother.' The sun's rays captured the lagoon-green lustre in her eyes. 'I should never have let you persuade me into coming back. I knew it wouldn't work.'

'Let's sit in my car and talk about it.'

'There's nothing to talk about. Just let me go.'

Paul tightened his grip on Maggie's arm. She tried to pull herself free but he was far stronger than her. Reluctantly, she allowed him to guide her across the factory yard and through the main gates to where his car was parked. Unlocking the passenger door, he gently, but firmly, pushed her inside. 'Please, Maggie, don't get out. Just listen to what I have to say.'

Maggie felt an overwhelming tiredness sweep through her body, her fighting spirit dissipating along with her anger. As Paul pushed a clean white handkerchief into her hand, Maggie noticed, vaguely, the initial *P* sewn in navy blue cotton on one corner of the soft linen. It woke a distant memory of dark blue squares, which didn't show stains or dirt, were easier on the eye, always carefully ironed even though they were rarely to be seen by folk at home. They never displayed any initials to indicate the owner's name, should anyone have the remotest interest. Martha had always made sure that Terry and John had at least half a dozen in their kitbags, when they went to sea; yet, it was normal practice at sea to use pieces of rag to wipe dirty, greasy faces.

Maggie dabbed her eyes then offered the handkerchief to its owner.

'No, you keep it,' Paul insisted.

Maggie remained silent, squeezing the snow-white cloth in the palm of her hand.

'I can only apologise for my mother, Maggie. Her behaviour was inexcusable. I know you won't want to come back to work for me at the office. I understand that and don't blame you. What will you do now?'

Maggie struggled to answer. Their closeness made her uneasy. 'I don't know. Go back to the agency, I expect. But, I doubt they will want me back. Not without a reference.' She glared at him. 'But, that's not your problem, is it?'

Paul studied her for a moment. 'I have a proposition to put to you, Maggie. Something to think about over the weekend.'

Maggie looked at him in surprise.

'I am looking for someone I can trust to look after my son during the school holidays, whilst I'm at work. I wondered if you could help me out. I would be very grateful.'

Maggie was completely taken aback.

'I'm a secretary, not a nanny.'

'I know that, Maggie, but it could help both of us. It would only be on a temporary basis, of course, whilst you are looking for another job.'

'Do you really think your mother would allow me to look after her grand-child? She hates me.'

Paul ignored the accusation, except to say, 'It has nothing to do with her. And, besides, she doesn't really like children.'

Maggie looked at him, not knowing what to say, for a moment., then asked, 'Who usually looks after your son?'

'Brenda, or she did until a week ago. She also cleaned for me three times a week and prepared evening meals. Unfortunately, she had to leave because her mother's ill and needs to be looked after. I will now either have to bring Kenny to work with me when he's not at school, or find someone to look after him. That's why I am asking you to help me.' Paul hesitated and studied her again. 'He's very easy to deal with, Maggie. Will you think about it and let me know your decision on Monday?'

'I'll think about it. But, I really don't feel I can help you.'

'Thank you, Maggie.' Paul smiled. 'And, by the way, you wouldn't be expected to do any housework or cooking, apart from lunch for Kenny and, of course, yourself.' He turned away from her and started up the engine. 'I'll take you home now.'

He stopped the car at the top of Maggie's street. She had insisted that he did so; it would attract less gossip. But, because her mind was in turmoil as she stepped out of the car, Paul politely holding the door open for her, she didn't notice that she was being observed. Mrs Adamson had a peculiar knack of being at a particular place at the right time, always to her advantage, not her victim's.

As Maggie walked slowly home, she could not stop thinking about Paul; she could still feel the stifling closeness as they sat side by side in his car; his aftershave lingered in her nostrils. When she entered the kitchen, Nora looked up at her in surprise. It was early afternoon. Martha, as usual, was sitting in her chair staring vacantly into space.

'You're home early, Maggie. Do you want a cup of tea? It's freshly brewed.'

'Thanks Auntie Nora.' Maggie sat at the table, opposite her aunt, struggling to appear normal.

But, Nora knew her niece too well. 'Is there something the matter, lass? Aren't you well?'

Maggie hesitated, keeping her head down. 'I've walked out of McKenzie's. Sacked myself, you could say.' Trembling, but with a modicum of triumph, she looked up at Nora and added, 'I didn't give that bitch, Kathleen McKenzie, the pleasure of telling me to go and not come back.'

She proceeded to relate the morning's events. When she came to the end of her story, she stared at her aunt in amazement. 'I can hardly believe that Paul McKenzie wants me to look after his son, even on a temporary basis. I told him that I was a secretary, not a nanny, but he still wants me to do it.'

'Well, Maggie, if you think about it, he does have a point. You could look after his son during the coming school holidays and, at the same time, be looking for a permanent job. That way, you would still be earning some money.' Nora paused. 'But, where does Mrs McKenzie fit into this? Surely, she's going to have a lot to say about it. We are talking about her grandchild.'

'She doesn't like children very much, apparently, surprise, surprise. She's not very interested in her grandson.. In any case, Paul insisted that it had nothing to do with her.'

'There is another point about all this, Maggie,' Nora said, gently. 'Correct me if I'm wrong but I think you are more than a little bit interested in Paul McKenzie. I mean in a romantic way. Am I right?'

'I don't understand myself, Auntie Nora.' Maggie had sidestepped her aunt's question, not wishing to commit herself to the truth.

They sat chatting at the table for a while then Nora looked at the clock on the mantelpiece and stood up. 'You finish your tea, Maggie. I'm going to bring in the washing.'

Before Maggie could argue, there was a loud banging on the front door. They looked at each other, curiously. 'Who on earth can that be?' Nora said. Maggie made a move to leave the table. 'I'll answer it, Maggie. You stay where you are,' Nora insisted. She left the room.

Keith's angry voice echoed through the house. He was shouting and swearing, demanding to see Maggie. Nora was trying to calm him down. 'She's having a lie down because she's not very well.'

'I don't believe you. I demand to see her.'

'It's all right, Auntie Nora. I'll deal with it.' Maggie was standing behind her in the doorway, trembling. Nora moved to aside. 'Demanding to come in won't get you anywhere, Keith,' Maggie told him, angrily. 'And there's no chance of you doing so in the state that you're in. I'll talk to you later; after you have calmed down.' She started to close the door.

Keith held it back with his hand. He spoke to Nora through the opening. 'I'm sorry if I've upset you.' He looked at Maggie again. 'I only want to talk to you,'

Maggie hesitated. 'I'm not letting you come into the house if you are going to frighten my mother by shouting. She's asleep.'

'I won't.'

Maggie reluctantly led Keith in and through to the front room. Neither of them sat down; they stood facing each other.

Keith forgot his promise; his temper flared again. 'What's going on between you and that trawler owner scumbag? Why was he bringing you home in his fancy car?'

Maggie was taken aback. Keith must have seen her getting out of Paul's car at the top of the street. But, she was puzzled. Why hadn't he confronted her then? 'What I do is my business,' she said furiously. 'But, as it happens, I've left McKenzie's; walked out of the office for good. Paul insisted on giving me a lift home because he knew that his mother had upset me. That's all there was to it.'

Keith's face relaxed slightly. 'So, you're not working there anymore?' 'No, I've just told you. I've finished working at the factory.' Maggie did not mention Paul's proposition. 'But, it has nothing to do with you,' she repeated. 'Whatever I do in my life, Keith, is my concern, not yours nor anyone else's. I've lost count of the number of times I've told you that but you don't seem to get the message.' She paused, then added, 'I want you to go now. If you come here shouting and swearing any more, I won't let you in. And, I'll certainly never speak to you again. Do you understand? Are you taking in what I'm saying, this time, Keith?' Maggie suddenly felt very tired and emotionally drained. The day had gone from bad to worse; she had had enough..

Keith looked at her, but said nothing, He allowed her to lead him to the front door. He turned and said, 'Mrs Adamson was, obviously, wrong. I'm sorry if I've upset you, Maggie.' She was momentarily taken back. He had said sorry twice in the space of a few minutes. It was not a word that came easily to him.

'What has she to do with all this?' Suddenly, it hit her. Mrs Adamson had seen her get out of Paul's car and could not wait to pass on the news to Keith. 'That bloody woman wants hanging.'

Keith left the house. Maggie closed the door with a loud bang, forgetting that Martha was frightened easily by noises. But, this time she did not wake up. Nora had been in the backyard, holding the kitchen door ajar, waiting for Keith to go. She came in and closed the door behind her. Her eyes were clouded.. 'Are you all right, Maggie?'

'I'm fine, thanks, Auntie Nora, no thanks to that nosey cow, Mrs Adamson. She saw Paul dropping me off at the end of the street. Everyone will know now. The gossips will have a great time pulling me to bits.'

'No, not all of them, lass, they know whose side you're on.'

Chapter 9

———————

The following Tuesday morning, Maggie wended her way apprehensively down the long winding path leading to Paul's home. It seemed endless. It was, compared with the small terrace where she lived. She asked herself, for the third or fourth time, how on earth she had managed to get herself into such a situation. I must be mad, she thought to herself.

When she reached the end of the drive, she was confronted by a large sprawling bungalow, set amid beautifully kept lawns and a diorama of spring flowers, which would do justice to any artist's paintbrush. Daffodils, in clumps, moved from side to side, dancing to the hidden melody of the gentle spring breeze. Occasionally, a few remaining clusters of snowdrops were to be seen sheltering under the golden petals and long narrow green leaves of the daffodils. The sun's rays accentuated the myriad colours flanking the path as the new season's blooms flaunted themselves. The trees' and bushes' bare winter shoulders were dressed in a gossamer shawl of pale green, newly formed leaves.

Before Maggie had time to ring the bell, the door opened. Paul was standing with a relieved smile on his face. 'Hello, Maggie, I wasn't sure that you would come. But, I'm very pleased that you have. Come in.'

Kenny was standing almost hidden behind his father but, as Paul helped Maggie with her coat, he came into view. He smiled at her. 'You're the lady we saw on the quay.'

Maggie was taken aback. Paul looked embarrassed. He ignored his son's remark.

'Kenny, this is Maggie. I think you met her once at the office. She is going to look after you whilst I am at work. Say hello to her.'

'Hello, Maggie.'

Beautiful blonde curls framed the boy's oval face. His innocent hazel eyes stared back into hers through thick, long lashes. But her memory of seeing him that early winter's morning was vague. It was his father's face that she remembered most clearly from that day; even though he had been standing fifty yards or more away from her across the quayside, almost hidden in the swirling snow and the dim mist. That one surreal moment had changed Maggie's life, perhaps forever; she had allowed him to intrude into her heart, her soul.

She smiled back at the young boy. She recalled the morning he came into the office soon after she started working for Paul. It had only been for a minute. Paul had called to pick up his diary. He was taking Kenny to school.

Maggie was suddenly aware that Paul was looking at her, enquiringly, as they stood in the hall. 'I'm sorry. What did you say?'

'Nothing much,' Paul replied, smiling. 'Only that Kenny will show you where everything is. You can always ring me at the office if you have any problems. But, I'm sure you won't have.' He turned to Kenny. 'Don't forget what I told you. You must be good for Maggie and help her.'

'I will, Daddy.'

'Thank you again, Maggie. I'll go now and leave you two to get to know each other better. I'll see you both at four o'clock.' Paul turned and left.

'Daddy said that I have to show you around the bungalow.'

'Yes, that's right, he did,' Maggie replied, laughing. She was beginning to relax. 'You lead the way, Kenny, and I'll follow.'

'I'll show you my playroom first, Maggie. I have hundreds of cars. And a train set.'

'I bet your daddy likes playing with them, doesn't he?' Maggie imagined them laughing together, heads bent close as they enjoyed each other's company..

'Yes, when he's not at the office. He said that you don't work for us anymore, Maggie. Don't you like us?'

'Of course, I do, Kenny, otherwise I wouldn't be here now, would I?'

'I suppose not.'

'It had nothing to do with not liking anyone,' Maggie said. 'Sometimes things don't workout as we want them to, when we are grownup. We don't always agree with each other and we need to move on.'

Kenny appeared to accept Maggie's explanation. She had a feeling, however, that it would not be long before he was questioning her again. He was, obviously, a bright child; quick and inquisitive.

As they walked around the bungalow together, Maggie felt as if she was trespassing. Everything looked immaculate. There were four bedrooms; one was used as a playroom, Paul and Kenny had one each, and the fourth one was kept as a guestroom. When Kenny opened Paul's bedroom door, Maggie could not bring herself to step inside. It was private. Most probably the room he had shared with his wife, who had died during a severe asthmatic attack, possibly in this particular room. Maggie closed the door gently.

'Shall we play in the garden? It's lovely and sunny out there. A shame to stay indoors,' Maggie said; she needed some air.

'I'll show you my swing,' Kenny offered. He rushed to the door at the back of the bungalow.

Maggie marvelled at the perfection of the lawn; the amazing array of colour in the flowerbeds and the varying pinks of the spring blossom on some of the trees and bushes.

She allowed Kenny to lead her into the play area of the garden. There was a slide, a seesaw, a double swing and a small roundabout. She had never experienced such luxuries as a child; she felt bewildered by everything she was seeing. But, she was also enjoying herself.

Every now and again, Maggie remembered the trawlermen and, unintentionally, compared the way Paul and his son lived with that which the trawlermen endured at the Arctic fishing grounds. All those men could look forward to was a profitable voyage and a safe journey home; God willing. Paul came home every day to a life of comfort and warmth. Maggie immediately put the criticisms out of her mind. She felt guilty. She was here to look after Kenny. She had agreed to do that.

'Come on,' she said, laughing. 'I'll race you to the swings.' She allowed Kenny to win.

He took hold of one of the ropes and held it out to her. 'You sit next to me, Maggie. We'll see who can get the highest.'

Soon, they were both laughing as they swung their legs underneath their seats in an effort to propel themselves upwards as far as they could go. Maggie started to sing. 'Higher and higher, up we go. Then lower and lower, down we go. The sky is blue, the ground is brown, who will reach the highest?'

Suddenly, Kenny screamed. One of his ropes had broken. The seat collapsed and he tumbled to the ground. Maggie brought her swing to a sudden halt. Kenny was now lying on his side, his arm twisted under him; he was obviously in severe pain. She tried gently to move him. He screamed louder. The arm was either dislocated at the elbow or it was broken. Maggie remembered Katy having a similar accident a year or so ago. I mustn't panic she thought, struggling to keep calm. She debated who to call first; Paul or the hospital.

She looked down at the boy and stroked the back of her hand over his cheek. 'You are going to be all right, Kenny, so don't worry. I am going to ring your daddy now but it will mean me having to leave you for a minute. Do you understand?'

Kenny nodded slightly, looking deathly white.

'I'll be as quick as I can.' As she ran across the lawn to the house, a picture of Kathleen McKenzie flashed through Maggie's mind. She would be in her element when she knew what had happened and would seize upon the opportunity to cause as much trouble as possible for Maggie, even though the accident had not been her fault. Kenny had been her responsibility for less than an hour.

After telephoning Paul, Maggie rushed back to Kenny. 'Do you think, if I help you, you can manage to stand up, Kenny Then, we can go back to the house. You'll be more comfortable there. I'll try hard not to hurt you.'

She bent down and gently helped him to his feet. As she did so, she noticed that his shirt had become dislodged from his trousers. She stared at the exposed area of his waistline. She felt faint.

Trying not to hurt him, Maggie lifted the shirt a little bit higher; the mark was now clearly exposed, lying across the full width of his back. For a second, she told herself that it must have been caused by his trousers; they may have been too tight. Or, perhaps, it was a common birthmark. Maggie knew that there was no point in jumping to conclusions. But, she had seen that mark on many occasions in the past. How could she possibly forget what it looked like? As far as she was concerned it was unique. Passed down from father to son. Kenny was the baby she had given away soon after his birth. There was little doubt in Maggie's mind. But, she would have to find out for sure.

Nobody had ever said, or even intimated, at the factory that Paul and his wife had adopted a baby. Perhaps, it had been deliberately kept quiet; a family secret, to be kept as such, by order of Kathleen McKenzie.

She forced herself to concentrate on Kenny's injured arm and the acute pain he was suffering. She guided him as gently as she could towards the back door of the bungalow. 'I'm so sorry about this, Kenny. I thought you were safe.'

'It wasn't your fault, Maggie. The rope broke. I've fallen off the swing lots of times before today,' Kenny assured her,

'It was an accident, I know,' Maggie replied, ruefully, 'But, why did it have to happen today, of all days, when I'm looking after you. Your grandma will blame me.' As soon as she had said the words, Maggie regretted them. Kenny should not be brought into adult problems; especially those between herself and his grandmother. Maggie tensed slightly. I hope he doesn't tell Kathleen what I said, she thought..

'I won't let her blame you, Maggie,' Kenny said. 'How long will daddy be?'

'He'll be here very soon,' Maggie replied. She hadn't rung for an ambulance; Paul had told her that he would leave the office immediately. If necessary, he would take Kenny to the hospital, himself.

As they entered the bungalow, they heard Paul's car speeding up the drive, followed by the loud slamming of a car door. Maggie breathed a sigh of relief.

'Maggie? Kenny?'

'We're in here, Paul.'

He looked at his young son and bent down and kissed him on the forehead. 'I think I'd better take you to the hospital, Kenny. I know you are hurting a lot but the sooner we get there the better it will be for you. They will know what to do.'

At Paul's insistence, Maggie accompanied them to the hospital.

'Will you sit at the back of the car with Kenny, whilst I drive, Maggie?'

'Yes, of course, I will.'

'It wasn't *your* fault, Maggie,' Paul assured her. 'If it is anyone's, it is mine. I knew that the rope was old and probably weak. It would have broken at any time. So, you must not worry.'

Maggie put her arm gently around the boy's shoulders, struggling with her emotions. She wanted to hug him and tell him how much she loved him; how very much she had missed him. But, she had given up the right to do that when she signed the adoption papers. But, the mark he had inherited from his father had catapulted the past into the present.

For over seven years, Maggie had wondered who was bringing up her son. Were they kind to him; did they love him as much as she did; was he happy and healthy; would she know him if she saw him? Now, at last, the irony of the answers would seem to have been revealed. Paul, a trawler owner's son, and his wife, had adopted her baby; and, yes, he was loved and happy. There was little doubt in her mind that Kenny was, indeed, her son.

Maggie had harboured a deep hate for the trawler owners for so long; an inexorable determination to fight them and persuade them to acknowledge their responsibilities for their crews at sea; to change things for the better. Yet, unbeknown to her, her son had been living in the luxury and safety of a trawler family's home; the same family who had owned the doomed ships in which his father and grandfather had drowned at the Arctic fishing grounds. The trawler owners had robbed Terry and Andy of the joy of watching Andy's son progress from childhood to maturity.

And, an even more cruel hand had been dealt to Maggie; she had fallen in love with Paul McKenzie. He had no idea that she was Kenny's mother

As she sat next to Kenny in the back of Paul's car, Maggie resolved never to let these knew developments in her own personal life affect her campaign. After all, hundreds of fishermen, some as young as fifteen, had perished over the years; Andy, Terry and John were but a very small minority of those. She felt the responsibility to help other young fishermen today had been forced upon her shoulders; perhaps, it had always been her destiny.

For the moment, she would cherish this opportunity she had been given to be close to her son. Nobody need ever know that she was Kenny's mother; certainly not Kenny, himself. It was enough for her to know that he was both loved and cared for by Paul.

———

The following week passed in a blur for Maggie. A confused, yet happy state, which she knew could not last much longer. Kenny's arm was encased in plaster but not giving him much discomfort. He would be returning to school soon. Every day, Maggie had immersed herself in the wonderful warmth of having her son so close to her, taking care of him after his fall, hugging him occasionally, and wishing that she need never again have to leave him. At least, she now knew he was not far away.

———————————

On the Thursday morning, Maggie received a short note from the immaculate Miss Jackson. The agency had a vacancy for a temporary secretary to work in an office on the docks, commencing the following Monday. Would Maggie be interested? Kenny would probably be returning to school that day. Maggie would not be needed anymore. She had looked after him for nearly two weeks. She had two more days left to enjoy being with her son. She had temporarily put to the back of her mind the possibility that she could be wrong.

'What shall we do today, Kenny?'

'Shall we go fishing, Maggie? Daddy takes me, sometimes. I have a rod.'

'How can I refuse? Of course I will.'

Kenny ran out of the house towards the garage, his left arm in a sling. In his eagerness, he almost tripped on the path.

'Be careful. You'll get me into a lot of trouble if you fall again.'

' No, I won't, Maggie. I'm not going to fall and I won't let Grandma blame you, if I do,' Kenny laughed over his shoulder.

Maggie had been very careful not to bring Kathleen into any of her conversations with Kenny. As she waited for him on the drive, she heard the telephone ringing and rushed to answer it.

'Maggie, it's Paul. I am probably going to be very late home today. The St *Bartholomew* is missing and I want to hang around in case there's any news. Can you look after Kenny for me until I get back?'

Maggie's heart started to pound. She could not answer Paul immediately; she felt the familiar tightness in her chest and the rush of anger through her veins. But, she forced herself to remain calm. For, at the moment, nothing was certain. The *St Bartholomew* need not necessarily have been lost.

'Are you there, Maggie?'

'Yes, I am. Sorry, Paul. Don't worry about Kenny. I'll stay with him until you get home. You will let me know if there's any news, won't you?'

'Of course I will. And, thanks, Maggie.'

Maggie put the telephone back onto its rest; her mouth was dry. Not another one, please God, not again, she prayed. She was suddenly aware that Kenny was walking toward her on the drive, holding a fishing rod in his left hand and a bag under his other arm. He was looking worried.

'What's the matter, Maggie? Who was that on the 'phone?'

Maggie told him what Paul had said, as calmly as she could; at the moment, the *St Bartholomew* was only deemed to be missing; there could be any number of reasons for that. But, Maggie had heard those words so many times before. She wondered how many of the ship's crew she knew. She would have to be patient until she heard from Paul again.

'Everything's going to be all right,' she said to Kenny, with a confidence that belied her true feelings. 'But, I think it will be best if we stay at home, this afternoon, Kenny. Your daddy's going to let us know as soon as he has any news.'

'Is the *St Bartholomew* one of granddad's ships, Maggie?'

'No, it isn't, Kenny.'

'Daddy took me down to the quay to see it leave, once. When it was new.' Kenny started to cry. 'I don't want the men to drown.'

'I know you don't. Nobody does. Please don't cry. You must be brave; like the fishermen. All of us must.'

Maggie wiped the young boy's eyes then hugged him gently. One day, she hoped, he will see for himself the full horrors of what the men have to face at sea; but not yet. His tender years should not be marred by stories of death and gloom. But, perhaps in time, he will also appreciate the reasons for her campaign and would try in his own way to help improve safety on the family's ships.

The long awaited news from Paul came at half-past six; the *St Bartholomew* had gone down with all hands. The city was once again in mourning.

———————

Maggie set off for work the following Monday morning with a heavy heart and a deep burning rage flaming inside her. It was a beautiful sunny spring day; albeit quite cold, but she hardly noticed. She had had little sleep over the weekend. It was going to be very difficult for her to concentrate on work today, particularly in a strange office.

As she approached the riverside quay she was met with a sea of blazing colour. Everywhere, there was evidence of the deep grieving in the community. Maggie knew that the people's anger was yet to be demonstrated; that would come in the aftermath of the shock and sadness, and the consoling of the bereaved. Then the full force of their feelings would explode in the pubs and on the streets, but mostly on the premises of the trawler owners; and the language would be far more colourful and vibrant than any blooms on show today.

The wreaths decorating the quayside varied in shape and size: some in deep yellow roses proclaiming: Daddy, we love and miss you, set out in a cross; others saying, I love you, darling, written in rich red blooms, shaped like a heart; dozens of sprays and bouquets confirming how much the lost trawler men were loved and would be sorely missed. But, most people in the community held a strong belief that the men's spirits would remain with the bereaved forever; it gave them a great deal of comfort, which nothing could take away, not even the trawler owners.

Maggie felt no embarrassment as she wiped her eyes. She stood for a moment, allowing time for her to compose herself before reaching Faulkner and Sons' offices, which stood further along the quayside from McKenzie's. She felt a sudden surge of anger rising from her sadness. She lifted her head high and straightened her shoulders.

There would be no more tears today.

She turned and walked back along the edge of the quay. There was no way that she was going into work today; certainly not for another company of trawler owners.

Nora looked at her niece, anxiously. 'What are you going to do for money, love?'

Maggie glanced thoughtfully down at the fourth finger on her left hand; that bare empty place that should have borne the rings signifying the joining of two hearts and bodies. It seemed such a long time ago. Now, fate had dictated that she must move on.

'To sell your engagement ring would be a big step, Maggie, ' Nora said. 'Please, don't do anything you might regret later.'

Maggie looked up at her aunt and gave a slight smile. As usual, Nora had endeavoured to read her niece's mind; this time she was wrong. 'I'm not going to sell my ring. I'm going to pawn it, which is different. Andy would have understood. I know he would. I am going to need more money than I'll be able to earn at Atkins and I'll have to find it somewhere; but I will, I always do, ' Maggie said, confidently. 'I'll be getting paid nearly three pounds a week for working part-time, with the probability of extra hours, so I'm not really worried too much at the moment.'

Maggie had seen a notice in the window of Atkins, the local bookmakers, for a counter clerk. She had agreed to work from one o'clock until five o'clock every afternoon on weekdays. This arrangement suited her fine. She would have the mornings and evenings free to plan meetings and campaign. But, first, she must persuade the women in the community to give her their support, and men, if possible.

Chapter 10

Maggie turned over and checked the time; it was three o'clock. The alarm on the bedside table had woken her up. She had had a restless night thinking about the reception she and her friends might encounter at the quayside; the verbal abuse and ridicule from the men standing at the rails of their ships. But she was not afraid, only determined to succeed, hopefully with the help of many others.

There had been no problem enlisting Pat's support; nor that of Annie Price and Kitty Fields, both fishermen's widows, whose husbands had met their untimely end on the *St Bartholomew*, another wreck now resting on the sea bed; a cold, lonely graveyard, it's caretaker a greedy, unrelenting ocean. The four angry, strong-minded, young women were united with a common purpose. Maggie had been adamant that they would be able to persuade others to join their group. Tomorrow would be only the beginning, she had insisted; there would be many tomorrows to face, with a lot of dirt thrown their way from people who disagreed with what they were doing. She had encouraged them all to be positive; they would succeed in their aims because they believed in them and knew that they were justified to take their fight to the bitter end.

As she quietly opened the kitchen door, Maggie was surprised to find the light on in the room and Nora sitting at the table. 'What on earth are you doing downstairs at this time, Auntie Nora? Aren't you well?'

'I'm fine lass but I had no intention of letting you leave home without something inside your belly. Sit down. Your tea's poured out and your toast's already buttered. It won't take you long to finish it.'

Maggie, dressed in knee-length suede boots, a warm dark woollen coat and a red headscarf, which hid her auburn hair, tried not to let Nora see that she was anxious to be on her way. She only had five minutes to spare before leaving the house to join Pat at the end of the street. She did not want to keep her friend waiting. It was still dark, daylight being almost two hours away; the streets providing quiet, hidden corners for those individuals with their own criminal agendas. And, it was a long walk down Hawthorn Avenue. They needed to be on the quayside well before four o'clock. They were meeting Annie and Kitty at half-past three at the corner of Westdock Avenue. From there, they would make their way to the quayside.

Maggie poured some cold water into her tea to cool it down and drank it quickly. She picked up the toast and stood up. 'I'll eat this on the way, Auntie Nora. Pat will be waiting for me so I must go now.' She gave Nora a quick kiss on the cheek and a hug. 'But, thanks for thinking about me.' She hurried towards the door, picking up her gloves from the sideboard as she passed; there would be a bitterly cold wind blowing inland from the North Sea. The quayside held no shelter from the elements. She turned and smiled through a mouthful of toast. 'Love you, Auntie Nora. Kiss mam for me. See you later.'

'Bye, lass, take care.' Nora sighed and shook her head as she heard the front door close behind her niece.

———————————

Hurrying along the underground passage, which led to the docks, the loss of the *St Bartholomew* was the main topic of conversation. None of the friends was a stranger to grief. They were all fully aware of the devastation the loss of a loved one at the fishing grounds rent upon those left behind. Annie and Kitty were suffering most, at the moment. But, like hundreds of others in their position, they would quickly learn to cope.

'How're you both managing?' Maggie asked, one arm through Annie's. Kitty was holding on to Pat's. It was a pointless question but one that was always asked at these times; partly out of compassion, partly out of habit. The answers were always the same. There were no tears today, only a burning anger and a need to survive, fuelled by a savage desire for revenge.

'Mally's been very quiet since Bill went,' replied Annie. 'Mavis never stops talking; rarely about her dad. And, she's always laughing. I'm sure it's her way of covering up her real feelings. She was Bill's little girl. He worshipped her and she adored him.'

Nobody made any comment; none was needed. Merely listening to Annie was all that was required to provide a modicum of comfort. She was the oldest of the four friends, the recent tragedy having brought them closer together. Annie's brown woollen coat and green headscarf enhanced her thick, blonde curly hair, which was held in a rubber band at the nape of her neck. It had always been the envy of most of her friends. But, since losing Bill, nothing could improve the pallor of her skin and the dullness now inherent in her sapphire-blue eyes.

'What about you, Kitty? It's good to see you but are you sure you should be doing this, in your condition?' Pat looked anxiously at the young woman who was clinging to her arm, her swollen belly leaving no doubt as to her predicament.

Kitty was very popular with everyone because of her generosity of spirit and warm nature. She usually had a mischievous smile; not today. She was now grey-faced and showing signs of ageing, yet she was only twenty-nine years' old. She had been working part-time in McKenzie's fish factory for over two years, as well as bringing up her brood on her own, whilst her husband, Peter, was at sea. She had three children; twelve-year old twin boys, a two-year old little girl and another baby due in five months' time. There had been a constant stream of visitors to her home in the last week, everyone desperate to help.

'I'm fine, Pat. Don't worry. The lads are off school and looking after Rosie. They're used to babysitting. They know the score. And, she's no bother.'

As they walked along the quayside towards the lock gates, the night sky conceding to the dawn light, Maggie turned to her companions in astonishment. 'Am I seeing things? Is there a group of lasses walking towards us along the quayside?'

Not many women around the Hessle Road area had shown any real interest in Maggie's crusade, when she had tried to rally their support. An older woman had snarled at her, 'You're common, all that shouting and carrying on.' Another had called from across the road, 'Why can't you leave it to the lads, you silly bugger? They know what they're doing.' Maggie had ignored them. They would change their minds, soon enough.

'Surely, they won't be here to see their lads off,' Annie said, watching the newcomers. Few women would test fate by saying goodbye to their menfolk, either when they were leaving home or at the quayside; they might not come back. 'Perhaps, they're coming to join us,' she suggested.

'There's no chance of that or they would have let us know,' Maggie answered.

'I can see Rita Stephenson with them,' pointed out Kitty. 'Her Bob went down with my Bill. And, there's Rosie Kent. Her Tom was lost on the *St Christopher*.

Rita and Rosie were getting nearer, followed by two other women. Maggie recognised them as Mavis Woodhead and Lottie Robinson. They were both widowed when the *St Bartholomew* went down; the most recent tragedy. Maggie grinned. 'Perhaps, we have got through to *them*, at least. Come on, let's see what they've got to say for themselves.' She waved at the two women.

'We couldn't let you do it on your own, Maggie,' Rosie said, when she joined the group. Her face was pale and drawn; her eyes clearly demonstrated her wish for revenge. 'We've realised that you have got a point. It's time something was done before any more poor buggers lose their lives.' Rosie turned and gestured with her eyes and a brief nod of her head. 'Forget about those two over there. They're trying to make up their minds whether to join you or not; the stupid cows. They'll see sense soon enough.'

'Like Mavis, I've tried to get them to change their minds but it's been a waste of time,' Lottie said. 'It'll be a different story if their lads don't come back, God forbid. I wouldn't wish it on anyone.' She turned to Maggie. 'Right, where do we start? We're all yours.'

'First of all, I just want to say thanks to you all for joining me today.' It was hard for Maggie not to be emotional. At last, she was seeing signs of support. Anger had festered inside her for such a long, frustrating time. And, she was beginning to feel she would achieve something. 'As soon as the boats are near to us, I want you all to shout as hard as you can at the lads on deck but don't do anything stupid. If you see me doing something you think is really daft, you are *not* to copy me,' Maggie told them. 'Do you hear?' She stared at them all, her face set. They didn't argue. They had accepted her as their leader. But, they all looked puzzled.

Mavis ventured to ask her, 'You're not going to do something dangerous, are you, Maggie?'

'As I said before, do as I say, not as I do. Remember, you all have kids to think about.' A beautiful boyish face surrounded by blonde curls, flashed through her mind. Then it was gone.

'Please don't do anything silly, Maggie. It won't help our cause,' Pat insisted.

Maggie smiled but said nothing.

Whilst she had been welcoming the newcomers, outlining what she wanted them to do, the *White Warrior* had slipped quietly through the lock gates and with a single blast on her siren entered the murky brown water of the Humber without incident. The dawn had not yet broken through the night's dark and cloudy sky. For those left behind, there was the promise of a beautiful day.

The small fishing vessel was on the first leg of her long journey to the Arctic fishing grounds around Iceland. Unfortunately, the country had imposed an increase in fishing limits around its coastline some months before; they said it was to help conserve fish stocks. This claim infuriated Britain as well as other nations. But, Iceland was adamant. Now, apart from the severe weather conditions that the trawlermen had to face, there was also the threat from Icelandic gunboats.

The *White Warrior* was leading a line of six trawlers, each with a full complement of provisions, and a crew of young men ready to take their chances, whatever fate had in store for them. It was work and work meant money.

Unbeknown to her supporters, Maggie had anonymously rung the offices of the local Mail and the Fishing Herald the day before, to hint that there was possibly going to be a demonstration early the following morning, as the trawlers were passing through the lock gates into the Humber. 'You'll glean more information if you send reporters to the scene,' she had told them. The publicity would help the campaign.

The timing of the reporters' and the photographers' presence could not have been more perfect. The women had started to shout and jeer at the crewmen standing on the deck of the second trawler, the *White Swan*, as it was passing through the lock gates. Rosie noticed the men with camera equipment. She turned to Maggie in amazement. 'Did you know they were coming, Maggie?'

The others looked at Maggie wide-eyed. She didn't answer Rosie. She only grinned. 'Get on with the job. You're wasting time.'

The girls laughed.

The *White Swan's* siren cut loudly through the early morning atmosphere. Half a dozen members of the crew could be seen standing at the rail, ghostly images in the mist. One or two of them waved and grinned at the girls. Another shouted angrily, 'Get back home to your kids and your dollytubs. You're behaving like tarts, you silly sods.'

'Don't forget to run as fast as you can when you reach the bottom, lads. You're going to need all the luck you can get,' shouted Kitty. 'Spare a thought for my Peter.'

'And my Barry,' shouted Mavis.

Maggie took out a parcel from the inside of her coat. She opened it quickly and threw the contents at the men on deck. 'Take that with you, lads. That's what could happen to you; dead as a doornail. But, it hadn't any brains. What about you lot?'

Pat burst out laughing. 'How on earth did you manage to smuggle that stinking fish under your coat without us smelling it?'

Maggie laughed, ignoring the question, then took three whistles out of her pocket and gave one to Pat and another to Kitty; they were standing nearest to her. She kept one for herself. She wished she had thought of borrowing a loud speaker, although she had no idea who would own one.

Before she could use the whistle, she noticed two women approaching them. They were the last of the group already at the quayside when Maggie had arrived with Pat and Kitty. Their faces were familiar to Maggie but she could not remember their names. Until recently, the fishing community had lived mainly on the Hessle Road and surrounding area. New estates were now being built around the fringe of the city, where many people had already been re-housed.

'Hi, lasses, we've come to help you, if we can,' said the youngest of the two women. Her long dark hair was hanging in a plait nearly to her waist, her eyes were warm and gentle. Sadly, her classical features had been marred by chickenpox or some other childhood condition.

'I know your faces but...'

'I'm Olive Brown, Maggie' interrupted the woman. 'And she's Lizzie Rawson. She lives next door to me; her Jim's on the *St Lawrence*. The boat nearly missed the tide because the radio operator didn't turn up. She's worried to death. She's sure something's going to happen the ship.'

Lizzie was well rounded and endowed with a wealth of flesh across her chest; a soft, safe haven for a distressed child. She had two boys aged seven and four, and a girl aged six. She was several inches smaller than her companion. Like a lot of mothers, she earned extra housekeeping money by working in one of the fish factories; Westham's and Company.

'Well, you'd better get stuck in, both of you,' laughed Maggie. 'Or, them over there will have gone before we can leave our mark.' She nodded her head in the direction of the remaining three trawlers.

Inch by inch the *St Lawrence* made her way through the lock gates and into the deeper water of the river.

'You fools,' Lizzie screamed after the trawler. 'You shouldn't sail without a radio operator.' She hadn't known this was happening until after the trawler had left the dock. She was angry and upset. She turned to the others and said, 'I'd rather he hadn't gone. We'd have managed.' Nobody asked her how.

Jim should not have been aboard the *St Lawrence* that morning. He had missed sailing on his usual ship, the *Mary Magdalen*, the day before, because of an attack of diarrhoea and sickness. He had joined the S*t Lawrence* as replacement engineer.

'Don't go you silly bastards. Come back. Think of your wives and bairns.' The women's voices were blown back at them by the bitterly cold north-easterly wind, which had travelled across the North Sea from Siberia. Even though it was still springtime, it was still cold in the early morning air before the sun's warmth had had time to reach the ground.

In their efforts to attract the attention of the men on the decks, none of the women had noticed the group of about ten police officers, approaching them.

'Come on, girls. Back home with you. You're too pretty to be out here in this icy wind. The men are not taking any notice of you.'

Annie pushed the young policeman away. It was obvious that he had not been expecting such force emanating from the tiny slip of a thing, as he took hold of her arm. He almost lost his balance. 'Sod off and leave us alone,' she told him. 'We're not doing any harm. We're trying to help the lads.'

'Here, here,' Kitty agreed.

The girls were all trying to ward off the officers. One of the men looked down at Kitty's belly. 'You shouldn't be doing this, madam, not in your condition.'

'My husband has already been fed to the fishes and nobody but these lasses care enough to do something about it. So, don't tell me I shouldn't be here.'

Before anyone could stop her, Maggie leaped towards the deck of the fifth trawler, the *Blue Diamond;* she slipped on the damp concrete. A burly officer grabbed her and dragged her back, saving her from going over the edge into the murky water.

'Leave me alone, you bugger.' Maggie kicked and screamed.

'I'm arresting you for disturbing the peace...' The officer refused to let go.

Before any of the other women could try the same stunt as Maggie, the police officers formed a cordon alongside the quay.

Realising there was little more they could do, the last of the trawlers finally edging its way through the lock gates, Maggie decided to call it a day. Still held in the strong grip of the officer's hand, she shouted to the rest of her group. 'That's it for today, lasses. We've done what we can, until the next time. I'll talk to you all tomorrow. Thanks, everyone.' She grinned at the officer. 'You can do your worst but you won't stop us.'

The officer looked at her sympathetically. 'I'm going to let you go, this time. My brother was washed overboard in the Barents Sea, so I know how you feel, but this is not the right way to go about things. So, the next time you feel like taking the law into your own hands, think very carefully before you do. You might not be so lucky the next time. For one thing, that water's very dangerous.' He looked across at another officer. 'It's all right, Rob. I've given her a warning.'

Maggie snorted then, as the officer loosened his grip, she pulled her arm free. She grinned, sarcastically. As she did so, she was shocked to see a figure standing in the distance; watching her. Memories came flooding back of the last time she had seen Paul on the quayside in similar circumstances. It had remained a mystery to her why he had never broached the subject with her.

———————————

'What do you want, Paul? Why have you come here? If it's to ask me to apologise, then you're wasting your time.'

'No, Maggie, that's not the reason. Kenny has been asking why you haven't been to see him. He's missing you.' He hesitated. 'And, so am I.'

'But…'

'Can I come in Maggie? I can't stand talking to you on the doorstep.'

Perspiration was running down the back of Maggie's neck as she struggled to keep calm. She felt a warm trickle of moisture sliding along the furrow between her breasts. Her hands were hot and sweaty. Her heart was racing. Paul had never been to her home before.

Reluctantly, she led him into the kitchen. It was nothing like the immaculate room at his bungalow. No gleaming pans hung from the ceiling. No expensive crockery shone down from the tops of pine cupboards. But, that was not important; Nora kept the house spotlessly clean. She was sitting in an armchair reading the paper as Maggie and Paul entered the room. She looked up in surprise and started to rise out of her chair. Her dark eyes darted anxiously from one to the other.

'No, please, don't get up,' Paul told her. 'You must be Auntie Nora. Maggie has often spoken about you and how hard you work.'

'This is Paul, Auntie Nora. Paul McKenzie.'

'Hello. It's nice to meet you, Paul,' Nora replied, still looking anxious. 'I have heard a lot about you, too, from Maggie.'

'Not all bad, I hope,' replied Paul, smiling.

She did not reply.

Maggie opened her mouth to say something; but she was speechless. Nora immediately went to her aid. 'I'll put the kettle on,' she said. 'Take Paul through to the front room, Maggie, it will be more comfortable for you both in there.'

Maggie led the way into the room. She walked towards the window, wishing she could escape.

'Sit down, Maggie. You're making me feel uncomfortable.' Paul was smiling gently at her. 'And, don't worry. I haven't come to see you about what happened on the quayside, although I must say that there are less dangerous ways to make a point.'

'That's true if someone will listen. But, they won't. So, I'll do whatever it takes to make them,' Maggie retorted angrily. She was still standing near to the window.

'I'll listen, Maggie.'

Maggie studied him. She felt a powerful urge to move towards him. It was but a brief moment of weakness. She remembered Andy, her father and John, and the countless numbers of other victims of the trawling industry. She had fallen in love with Paul, a trawler owner's son, against her will. Now she must be strong and push him out of her mind, otherwise her efforts would all have been in vain.

'If it's nothing to do with what happened down at the quayside, then what is it? I'm busy. I have to attend to my mother.' It was a lie. Nora had washed and fed Martha earlier.

'I've already told you, Maggie. Kenny is missing you. We both are.' He paused for a moment, looking directly into her eyes. 'You must know how I feel about you, Maggie. And

I know you feel the same way about me. Your eyes say the words even if your mouth doesn't.'

'You are so wrong. I feel nothing for you.' Maggie saw Paul flinch.

'I don't believe you, Maggie. Look into my eyes and tell me again that you do not love me.'

Maggie looked at him and said, firmly, 'I do not love you, Paul. You should find someone to love of your own class.' Her heart was breaking but she had already chosen the path she was to take and there was no way back.

'I know there are a lot of problems to overcome before you can trust yourself and me, but I will help you,' said Paul.

'How? Can you persuade your father and the rest of the trawler owners, and most of all, your mother, that something has got to be done to make the trawlermen's jobs safer? So many have died because of the greed of the trawler owners; young men with families, your age and younger. You live in luxury while widows bring up their children in poverty. Where can the justice be in that? Don't you ever feel guilty?' The early afternoon sun through the window caught the deep lustrous green of Maggie's eyes making them sparkle.

'The answer is not as simple as that, Maggie. But, I will try to help, if I can. I promise.'

Nora knocked on the door and entered, hesitantly, with two cups of tea and a plate of biscuits on an old wooden tray. The walls were thin. Only whispers could ever be completely private in the Victorian terraced house. But, Nora asked no questions nor made any comments about what she must have overheard.

'Mr McKenzie is just leaving, Auntie Nora.' Maggie turned to Paul. 'I want you to go now. And, I can promise you that the fight will go on until we get what we want. No matter how long it takes.'

When she heard the front door close, Maggie sat down on the old settee and wept. Nora rested the tray, which she had been holding, on a nearby stool then put her arms around her niece and held her tight.

'Was I too hard on him, Auntie Nora? You must have heard us talking.'

'Yes, I heard. I couldn't help it. And, yes, perhaps, you were too hard on him but I really can't say for sure. But, it's easy to see that he's in love with you, Maggie. Whether or not it could work, who can say.'

Maggie pondered Paul's words: Kenny is missing you. We both are. And, I love you.

And, she was missing them, too.

———————

Later that day, as she picked up the Daily Mail from the hall floor, Maggie's eyes were drawn immediately to the headline:

WOMAN NEARLY DROWNED WHILST TRYING TO BOARD TRAWLER

Below the caption was a photograph. Maggie hardly recognised herself. She was gesticulating at the trawler as it made its way towards the lock gates. She looked scruffy and angry. If what Paul said was true, what does he see in me, she wondered. But, it was of no consequence now. She continued reading.

'We have taken this action today for the trawlermen who risk their lives every time they go to the fishing grounds. Unless something is done to improve safety, it won't be long before another boat is lost; more families left to mourn. The owners have got to be made to accept responsibility for the crew's welfare. At the moment, they don't want to know. They don't care.

Once again, a ship, the *St Lawrence*, has been allowed to go sea without a radio operator. The fact that the skipper has a certificate to do the job is of no comfort at all to the men's families. How can he be at the helm and take command of the ship if he has to repair radio equipment and send messages?

This is only the start of the battle and I can assure everyone it will continue until we get something done. Our campaign will not only take place at the quayside, it will also be on the docks and at the offices. Those at the top had better take note. We mean business. We'll go to the Prime Minister, himself, if necessary.'

Maggie put down the newspaper, satisfied with what she had read. A reporter had taken the statement from her before she left the quay; she had written it the night before when she got home from work.

The job at Atkins was suiting her perfectly, at the moment. She still had her engagement ring in its box, safely hidden in her bedroom. She was loathed to part with it but she would do so if she had to; particularly if she needed money to help her to continue the campaign. But, it would have to be a last resort.

Nora was now staying with Maggie and Martha permanently. 'To help look after my sister,' she had said. Maggie could now concentrate completely on other important matters.

The night before, she had dreamt of Paul. He was chasing her along the river's edge. She was running as fast as she could to get away from him but something very strong was holding her back. She looked down into the river, debating whether to jump into the water. She heard his voice calling, 'Don't do it, Maggie. Don't do it.' Kenny's face appeared, tears running down his cheeks. 'Please don't jump, Maggie.' Then, she heard Kathleen McKenzie's harsh voice, encouraging her, 'Yes, do it. Do it. Jump quickly.'

Maggie woke up in a sweat. Her heart was pounding. Realising it had all been a bad dream, she turned over and buried her face in her pillow and wept; for her son who knew her only as Maggie, and a love affair that could never be.

———————

Nora looked up from the stove as her niece entered the kitchen.

'You look tired, lass. Haven't you had much sleep?'

'I had a bad dream again, Auntie Nora. Paul was chasing me and...' She did not finish her sentence. Someone was banging at the front door. It sounded urgent. Martha, having been washed and dressed by Nora at six o'clock that morning, was sitting quietly in her chair until she heard the noise vibrating through the house. She cried out in alarm. 'Someone's coming to get me, our Maggie.'

'It's all right, mam, it's only someone knocking at the door. Nothing for you to worry about.' Maggie heard Nora talking to someone. Maggie recognised a woman's agitated voice.

'Is Maggie there?'

'Yes, come in.' Nora led Annie Price into the kitchen. 'Whatever is the matter, lass?'

Annie looked at Maggie and said, 'You, obviously, haven't heard the news.'

'What news?'

'The *St Lawrence* is missing. The offices on the dock can't make radio contact with it. Jim Rawson's an engineer on the ship.'

Maggie forgot how tired she felt.

'Not another one,' she said, not wanting to accept the possibility. 'I must go round to see how Lizzie is, Auntie Nora. Mam will be all right with you, won't she?'

'Of course she will, lass.'

'Are you coming with me, Annie?' Maggie asked her, as she quickly put on some shoes and grabbed her coat.

They dashed out of the house and hurriedly made their way along Hawthorn Avenue towards Lizzie's house. It stood on the front facing the road and was half way between Anlaby Road and Hessle Road. To some folk, it was deemed to be posh; large bay window draped with frilly cream-coloured nets and a small storm porch protecting the front door from the elements. A low wooden fence ensured that the neat front garden was kept private. Maggie and Annie went round to the back of the house and found the children playing in the small yard.

'Of course daddy's coming home, Molly. Don't talk like that again,' the eldest boy, Tommy, was saying firmly to his sister; she was only a year younger than himself.

Molly started to cry. Annie bent down and put her arms around the child's shoulders. 'There, there, luvvy, don't fret yourself. Your daddy will be coming home soon, I'm sure.' She stood up, leaving the child in Tommy's care, and went to join Maggie and Lizzie in the kitchen.

'Those bastards sent the men to sea without a sparks,' said Lizzie, her angry eyes wet with unshed tears. 'What if he doesn't come back, Maggie? What shall I do; three bairns to feed and no money. If the ship's gone down the men's pay will be stopped straight away; what about his bond bill?'

'Try not to worry too much, at the moment, Lizzie,' said Maggie. 'Wireless contact can be lost for as long as a couple of weeks before anyone hears from a ship. Probably, the skipper's found a good fishing spot and doesn't want the other skippers in the area to know about it. Anything can have happened.' She was trying to sound calm and positive but deep down she feared the worst.

The practice of leaving port without a radio operator was not illegal under the current Board of Trade regulations; nor was it uncommon. The skippers were trained to take responsibility for radio communication, if necessary. They also carried out repair work; but many people in the community argued that this was unacceptable. 'How can the skipper do two jobs a once? How can he lead his ship and radio for help at the same time, when the decks and bulwarks are covered in several inches of black ice and the ship's fighting mountainous waves? The safety of the crew should be paramount not the owners' pockets. But, nobody at the top ever wants to know.' The angry sentiments were always repeated, every time another trawler was lost.

'I'm going down to the docks to see if there's any news, Lizzie. Hopefully, there will be and it'll be good.' Maggie turned to Annie. 'Can you stay with Lizzie for a little while?'

'No,' argued Lizzie, tearfully. 'You get off, Annie. You have own bairns to think about.'

'I can stay for an hour, Lizzie. I'll make another brew and, hopefully, Maggie will be back with some good news before I leave,' insisted Annie.

As she hurried away from the house, Maggie bumped into Keith. 'I can't stop, Keith. I've to go down to the docks. The *St Lawrence* is missing.' A thought occurred to her. 'Has Pat gone to work on her bike?'

'I don't know. I'll go back and find out. If she hasn't, I'll ride it down the road next to mine and catch up with you.'

Maggie was running up Hawthorn Avenue towards Hessle Road, yet it seemed to be taking her forever to reach the end. She was almost there when Keith caught up with her. She had hardly seen him since their last argument about her looking after Kenny. Once again, she appreciated his support. And he would remember.

John Rawlings had not been pleased to find himself skipper of the *St Lawrence*. He usually captained the *Mary*

Magdalen. Unfortunately for him, he had had to give evidence in Court concerning the sudden death of a deckhand a few miles from home on his last trip on the *Mary Magdalen* and the case had finished a day late.

The *St Lawrence* had a bad reputation. It was built in 1953 and bought by Andersons in 1960. After a thorough overall, it had been pronounced safe and seaworthy and returned to duty. Soon afterwards, however, her performance was found to be generally unacceptable, fish quotas abysmal. The company had asked one of its top skippers, Arthur I'Anson, to take the vessel out and report back on any problems he encountered. Unlike other vessels I'Anson had captained, the *St Lawrence's* behaviour had given him much cause for concern. The ship rolled even in a swell; when the weather was not bad. She would drop suddenly for no apparent reason and, on one occasion, had nearly turned over. Skipper I'Anson had expected the worst but the ship had righted herself and he and his crew had returned home safely. However, I'Anson had concluded that the *St Lawrence* was a disaster waiting to happen. His report had been a verbal one, which suited both him and the owners. Rawlings had his livelihood to think about; if anyone, whatever their status, displeased the owners, they could be out of work for months. The owners, for their part, had made sure they had an escape route when requesting a verbal report only; they could say they were never fully informed of any problems, should there ever have to be an investigation.

Skipper Rawlings had agreed to take command of the *St Lawrence* for one trip only; the owners did not know that, only his wife, Mavis. If it meant he could be out of work for a while, so be it. It was better to be alive with no income than be eaten by crabs.

As the ship approached the fishing grounds, the weather took a turn for the worse. Winds were reaching nearly ninety miles an hour. The ocean was a cauldron of boiling froth.

White topped waves reached high to the dark beyond; they curled and bowed, orchestrated by the raging wind. And millions of gallons of water spewed over the bows of the ship, crashing across its slippery decks, before returning to the master; the demanding sea.

Below deck, the skipper struggled to repair the main transmitter, swearing and cursing; he seemed to have spent most of the trip up to now in the wireless room. True, he was qualified to take on the responsibility of a radio operator, if there was not one on board or if the man was ill, but maintenance and repair work was not part of that qualification. However, he felt he had sufficient knowledge to be able to carry out the necessary tasks; he had no choice.

The *St Lawrence* had first lost radio contact, albeit briefly, with the shore when the skipper had been talking to his wife soon after leaving the shelter of the Humber; transmission had returned, only to be lost again soon after. Since then, contact with other trawlers in the area had been brief and for short bursts only.

Alan Roberts, the ship's mate, who was a fully qualified and very experienced seaman, was in command of the vessel whilst Skipper Rawlings worked down below. Roberts had been out of work for six weeks prior to this trip, unable to find a skipper's job, for which he had been trained and certificated. The talk was that he had disagreed with Christopher Anderson, the trawler fleet's owner, because of an undisclosed matter. Roberts would not have been advised to his face that he had been given walkabouts for a while. It was an accepted fact by all crew members, even skippers, that the owners had the upper hand and, by a word in the right ears, could make sure the 'guilty' man was taught a lesson, however small his demeanour, by withholding work from him. More often than not the culprit never found out what he was supposed to have done.

At last, the fierce weather abating slightly, the gale-force winds allowing the ocean to breathe a little, the vessel reached an area off the coast of Iceland, outside the forbidden waters. Fishing commenced.

But, Skipper Rawlings had something knew to add to his problems; engine troubles. The vessel was now suffering from a severe lack of power; which was greatly hampering its speed. This was also seriously affecting shooting and hauling. The vessel should have been able to move at twelve knots but, instead, her top speed was only about ten and a half. Fish could not now be forced far enough down into the cod-end, thus allowing many to escape. The skipper took his frustration out on Jim Rawson, the chief engineer.

And the hurricane winds returned to test the small vessel, once more. She struggled head to wind, in an effort to ride out the storm but, even with engines at full ahead, meeting the waves head-on, the vessel was hardly moving. A less discerning skipper might have tried his luck by turning astern but John Rawlings knew better. It was far too risky. The trawler would be lifted broadside onto the brow of a wave into the full force of the blizzard. It could capsize and there would be little or no chance of survival for any of its crew, especially if the ship was unable to make radio contact with any other vessels in the area; or reach the Norwegian coastguards to call for help. The ship could be swamped whilst running with the waves; a small vessel, such as the *St Lawrence*, would have no chance of surviving in a heavy swell, particularly with her history. Her superstructure might not be strong enough to hold against the might of the sea; she could turn over and sink quickly to the bottom of the ocean. The troubles with her engines continued. Jim Rawson longed to be at home with Lizzie. The skipper promised his crew that they would return home safely to their families. They hoped he was right. But he was not God.

At last, the order came to clew-up. The men sighed with relief. The ship's performance had been a cause for concern throughout the whole trip. The amount of fish packed head to tail in ice in the pounds below was abysmal. John Rawlings was not a happy man.

———————————

Chapter 11

Maggie studied the small blue box she was holding; memories came flooding back. Nestling inside was a physical reminder of the special love there had been between her and Andy. He had put as much away as he could on his return from each fishing trip, "to *buy something very special for my girl*," he had told her, when they became engaged.

Hesitantly, she took the ring out of its box and gently ran her finger over the tiny, glittering stone. Its brilliance caught the green depths of her eyes, causing them to sparkle; like the rays of the sun touching a crystal-clear tropical waterfall.

Mr Iveson, the local pawnbroker, a kindly man who was looked upon by the community almost as a friend, would recognise the ring's value; not a fortune by a trawler owner's standards but a tidy sum, nevertheless, to Maggie now that her savings had almost gone. She returned the ring to the safety of its box then went to the cupboard under the stairs for her coat. Before putting it on, she placed the box in one of the pockets. She then left the house, quietly closing the front door behind her in order to avoid being questioned by Nora, who was upstairs dressing Martha. It was best that she was not aware of her niece's decision. She would have insisted on withdrawing some of her own savings. Maggie would never have agreed to that. Nora had done more than enough for her and Martha, always insisting, when Maggie brought up the subject, that she would not have it any other way.

It was now early September and Maggie could feel a distinct chill in the air as she walked along the Avenue. She checked her pocket once again. The box was still there. As she passed Lizzie's house she thought about her friend and her husband, Jim. He still refused to talk about his ordeal on the *St Lawrence*, or how he came to be the lone survivor when the ship went down off the coast of Iceland; not even to his wife, Lizzie. The vessel's owners were also waiting to hear Jim's story but, for the moment, he had retreated into himself, putting the episode out of his mind completely. Even his mates in the pubs could not persuade him to talk. Lizzie had confided with her friends that he rarely spoke to her about anything, nowadays. 'Be patient, he will tell you what happened when he is ready,' the doctor had advised her, when she visited the surgery.

Maggie had almost reached the end of the Avenue when a black Ford car stopped slightly ahead of her. Her heart lurched then started to race. Her hand reached down to her pocket; a reminder of where she was going and why.

'Can I give you a lift, Maggie?' Paul called to her as he stood near his car, holding the front passenger door open.

'No, thanks, I don't need one. I haven't far to go.' Maggie regretted looking at him. Every time she felt she could start living her life without him constantly being in her thoughts, he came back to haunt her. 'Please leave me alone Paul. I don't want to talk to you.' She started to walk again, head held high.

'I'm only offering you a lift, Maggie, that's all. I'll take you to where you are going then leave you.'

She stopped and looked at him again.

He smiled at her with that enigmatic warmth which could touch her heart without any kind of physical contact; she felt weak. 'You don't even have to talk to me whilst I'm driving if you don't want to,' he said, smiling.

'I really don't need a lift, Paul, but thanks for offering.' She turned away from him, not wanting him to see the effect he had on her; she started to walk quickly.

'Well, if you insist, I'll let you be on your way. I only wanted to help,' Paul called after her.

The disappointment in his voice halted Maggie in her tracks She felt guilty. It seemed that he genuinely wanted to help. She, warily, turned back and looked at him. But, this time, she kept a steady heart and her emotions controlled. Paul had closed the passenger door and was walking round to the driver's side of the car.

'I do appreciate your offer, Paul, but I was telling the truth. I really don't have much further to go. In any case, I feel it is best for both of us if we don't have any contact, especially as things are at the moment with the campaign. We come from different worlds, Paul. You're upper class, I'm working class. The two don't mix.'

'Class doesn't matter, Maggie. People do. And, you must know how much I love you.'

Maggie did not answer. Her hand once more reached into her pocket and felt for the ring box. 'How's Kenny?' she asked. She was suddenly filled with an overwhelming sadness; a deep sense of loss.

'He's fine and often asks about you. He would love to see you, Maggie.'

'I have to go or I'll be late. I'm sorry. Bye, Paul.' She turned and quickly walked away from him, wiping the back of her hand across her cheek where a stray tear had fallen. Self-pity was not allowed. She must keep her mind focused on the battle to be fought and, hopefully, won.

Paul drove by her without looking back.

After visiting Mr Iveson, she would be able to pay for the hire of the Victoria Hall. That was what was important, at the moment. Tomorrow was going to be an important day. Jack Lewis had agreed to speak at the meeting and answer questions.

Never before had Hull been touched by such a display, en masse, of anger and frustration, total unity of minds, all wanting revenge. Two ships had gone down over the past few months alone, with the loss of all members of the crew, bar one; Jim Rawson. Wives, mothers, sisters, lovers, left bereaved and betrayed by those whose responsibility it was to keep their men safe; the trawler owners. Raw emotion was evident, almost tangible, in the hall.

Maggie stood on the platform and surveyed the sea of faces down below. There were no empty seats to be seen. In the aisles, youngsters played and giggled around the feet and legs of adults; almost lost in the melée, their chatter mingling with the cacophony around them. People were standing at the back of the hall, squashed amongst prams and pushchairs. Headscarves of all colours bobbed about along the rows as mothers endeavoured to coax young children into being quiet; at the same time, they engaged themselves in conversation with their neighbours. Pat's Katy was sitting on the front row. The seat had been kept for her so that she would not be far away from her mother. Since John died, Katy had been anxious to have her mother nearby at all times. She waved to Maggie.

To her surprise, Maggie saw a number of male faces in the crowd, men no longer isolating themselves from the women. Such a sight would have been unthinkable a short time ago.

She turned to Pat, who was sitting next to her. 'I've waited for this day for such a long time,' she whispered. She grinned at the others sat at the table: Lizzie, Rosie and Alice. Looking away, she noticed a couple of men at the back of the room with cameras on their shoulders. A smile of satisfaction spread across her face. She dug Pat in the ribs and pointed in the direction of the men. Maggie had rung the offices of the Daily Mail and the Fishing Herald the day before to let them know that the meeting was going to take place. They had not let her down. Publicity was invaluable to the women's campaign; hopefully, it would make the trawler owners very nervous. Maggie waved to the reporters to let them know she had seen them. As she was doing so, she noticed Jack Lewis pushing his way down one of the side aisles. Following him was a tall, well-built man of about the same age. Maggie recognised his face from the Daily Mail; it was Roy Morgan, the local representative for the Transport and General Workers Union. She gave a deep sigh of relief. They were late but at least Jack had kept his promise to come. And, he had managed to persuade Roy to join him.

Maggie stood up and rapped on the table as the two men ascended the platform. 'Can you all now be quiet, please. We are about to start the meeting.'

A hush fell across the hall; the only sound to be heard was that of a young child crying. Jack and Roy took their seats at the centre of the table. Maggie looked at them and smiled. 'First of all, I would like to welcome Mr Lewis and Mr Morgan and to thank them for taking the time to join us today. Let's give them a big hand, shall we?' The response was loud and united; the tumultuous roar from the crowd blocked out the tearful voice of the child.

Jack Lewis stood up and returned Maggie's smile. 'It's Jack and Roy.'

Maggie grinned. 'Jack and Roy it is.'

Turning back to the audience, Jack opened the meeting. 'I would like to say thank you to every one of you for coming here today and also to Maggie for giving Roy and I the opportunity to talk to you and answer questions, if we can. I must admit that I am overwhelmed with the warmth of your response. Hopefully, we can soon start looking forward to improved safety for our trawlermen, when they are at the fishing grounds. But, I must warn you all to be very patient. These things can take a long time to come to fruition.'

'Our men haven't got time to bloody wait, Jack,' one woman shouted.

'That's right, Jack,' called another voice from somewhere at the back of the hall. 'My husband is at sea now. Hopefully, he'll be back.'

'Here, here.' Others joined in.

'Maggie stood up and banged loudly on the table. 'Please keep quiet everyone or you won't be able to hear what Jack has to say. When he's finished, you will be able to ask him questions and have your say.' The noise died down almost immediately. 'And, let's have no swearing today, if you don't mind, ladies. It won't do our cause any good,' she added, grinning. 'Let's give a good impression to the press. We have to show them at the top, the trawler owners, that we're as good as them, any day.' Maggie's ears pricked sharply, as the vocal response from the auditorium rang out so loudly, it touched the nerves. She sat down.

'I'm really proud of you, Maggie,' Rosie whispered. 'You sounded so confident.'

'I'm learning,' Maggie replied. She turned to Jack. 'I'm sorry about the interruption, Jack but I think it's safe for you to continue now."

Jack nodded then went on with his speech. 'I do appreciate your fears but we are talking about very big changes which are needed to be made. These cannot happen overnight. But, I promise you all that I shall be working as hard as I can to get results, along with Roy. And we shall, of course, keep everyone fully informed, at all times, of any progress that is made.' Jack gave the audience a moment to express their appreciation before continuing. 'I have recently been holding discussions with the Transport and General Workers Union into the ways we can force the trawler owners to take full responsibility for the safety of the men on their ships. To that end, I have spent many hours over the last couple of weeks, in the company of Roy, discussing how best we can go forward. We have yet to speak to all of the trawler owners but, for a start, we have an appointment with Christopher Anderson next Thursday morning and one on Friday the following week with Paul McKenzie, the son of Lawrence McKenzie; his father is, unfortunately, in hospital at the moment.'

'Oh, what a shame,' someone shouted. Loud laughter and booing filled the auditorium. Maggie had a momentary feeling of shame that they could have so little feeling for another human being; someone like Kenneth McKenzie. They did not know him. He was a kind man. But, many people in the audience, and Maggie herself, had lost loved ones on his ships; so they had every right to be angry and devoid of compassion.

Jack ignored the interruption. 'We shall, of course, welcome Maggie's support at those meetings, and perhaps one other member of the committee. Roy is going to speak to you all, briefly, now. After that, we would be more than pleased to hear the views of anyone here today. Thank you. I give you Roy. ' He sat down. The audience clapped, once again.

Maggie was sitting frozen in her seat as she took in the full implications of Jack's words. He had never said anything about her taking part in meetings with the trawler owners; particularly, with Paul. She would have to refuse Jack's offer; try to find an excuse not to go. There was no way she could sit calmly at a table opposite Paul. Pat or one of the other committee members would have to take her place. As Roy talked, Maggie could hear his voice from afar but could not take in anything he was saying. When he mentioned her name, it did not register with her.

'My first thoughts, when I heard about Maggie's campaign, were of disbelief and, I must confess, some amusement.' The audience interrupted angrily. Roy raised his hand to quieten them. 'Be patient,' he told them. 'Let me finish. You'll see that I am on your side. I asked myself, what could a group of women possibly achieve? And, what was the point of it all? Men have gone to sea for hundreds of years, taking their chances against the elements. That's what trawlermen do, whilst the womenfolk stay at home and look after their families.' Once more, the audience had become impatient. Heavy boots and shoes hammered on the wooden floor; voices jeered, drowning out Roy's voice.

Maggie hammered again on the table. The din had brought her back to her senses; to where she was and why she was there.

'It's okay. I admit I was wrong,' continued Roy, having raised his voice in order to be heard over the babble. 'I am not ashamed to say it.' The hall had become quiet again apart from one or two children crying, probably because they were frightened. 'What right have the trawler owners to risk their crew's lives? I wonder how many of them have braved the Arctic waters; how many of them have ever struggled to keep their balance on decks slippery with icy water and gutted fish; how many have suffered frostbite from hacking away at several inches of ice on the bulwark, whilst struggling against hurricane winds and blizzards, which prevail at the fishing grounds. At the end of the day, how many of the trawler owners really care about what the crews suffer on their behalf? None, I should think.' He had to shout louder and louder to be heard.

Roy had whipped his audience to a frenzied outpouring of anger. Most people were on their feet; men, women, even children, cheering and baying for revenge.

'You're right, Roy. None of the buggers care,' someone shouted from the back of the hall.

'Why don't you ask the bastards, Roy?'

Maggie's rule regarding swearing in the meeting had been ignored. And, for the moment at least, she had forgotten about Paul and the meetings that had been arranged. She stood up and once again hammered on the table. 'Please sit down everyone and let Roy finish what he has to say. You'll all get your turn in due course.' Maggie had shouted but still the people's voices driven by raw emotion filled the room. Jack stood up. The deep resonance of his voice finally reached their ears. The hall became quiet again. Jack and Maggie returned to their seats.

'I have almost finished,' said Roy. 'I merely wanted everyone to know that I do understand what the women here are fighting for and I'm full of admiration for you all. Like Jack, I shall be working as hard as I can to get the trawler owners to listen to what we have to say. Hopefully, after the meetings scheduled with them, we'll be able to report back to you all very soon on any progress reached and how we think we should go forward in the future. Thank you all for coming here today and please, everyone, try to be patient. Jack and I are on your side.' Roy sat down to rapturous applause.

Maggie, fully in control of herself again, stood up. 'Thank you, Roy.' She faced the audience. 'You can now ask questions but please keep them brief so that other people can have a turn. And remember, there hasn't to be any swearing. We want to give a good impression to the press.' She sat down.

Jack took the stage. 'Right, who wants to ask a question?'

'I do,' shouted one woman. 'Why is there a skipper's wife on the committee? Her husband's not one of us he's in the gaffer's pockets.'

Alice Foster stood up; a diminutive figure next to Jack, standing around five feet tall and slimly built. 'I've already answered that question when I first joined the committee. But, I'll answer it again. My husband, like all the skippers, belongs to the owners. Our men are given a job to do, to the best of their ability. If a voyage lands in debt, the skippers lose money, just the same as the rest of the crews. If a ship goes down, so do the men – that includes the skipper. My husband is fishing somewhere off Norway, at the moment. He doesn't know I'm here today. The chances are he'll be furious with me. He'll say that women shouldn't meddle in men's affairs. Well, lasses, I'm with you. I want my husband back home, safe and sound. It is time to make a stand and demand that the trawler owners face up to their responsibilities. Winter is approaching and already conditions are deteriorating in the Arctic Circle. We have got to act now. I know that deep-sea fishing will always be very dangerous but there are many ways that safety can be improved. That is all we are asking of the owners.' She turned to return to her seat. The audience roared; not against her, but in support. She appeared to have won them over.

'I wouldn't want to be in your shoes, Alice, when your Ray gets back,' whispered Rosie.

'I think I'll leave home before then,' Alice grinned. But, it was not a laughing matter, not when faced with Ray's violent temper.

'Who's next?' Jack asked the audience.

'I lost my husband and my brother, both on Anderson's ships. Nobody from the company ever came to see me or our family. They sent the Pastor from the Bethel round, as usual. I don't think Anderson's, the bastards, cared.' The woman was standing up near the front of the auditorium with tears running down her face. She sat down, wiping her eyes, her two children looking on.

Another young woman stood up with a baby in her arms. 'Why do the trawler owners wait so long before investigating, when they haven't heard from a ship for several days? They always have an excuse. My husband was on the *St Lawrence*.' She sat down.

'This is one of the issues we'll be taking up with the trawler companies,' replied Jack.

A man of around fifty years' old stood up. His grey hair was receding, his cheeks ruddy from working in all weathers. 'Look,' he said, waving his hand around in the air for everyone to see; there were two fingers missing. 'My hand was trapped in a winch during a blizzard. I was taken into Reykjavik and flown home. I haven't worked since then. My money was stopped the day this happened. I was told it was my own fault. Nobody at McKenzie's was interested.'

Maggie's thoughts immediately went to Kenneth McKenzie and Paul. The man's remarks showed them in a very bad light. And, yet, Maggie saw another side to them. But, she could not allow sentiment to affect her thinking. She had a job to do. Huge responsibilities lay heavy on her slim shoulders. And, after all, she was the one who had started the campaign.

The meeting carried on for nearly two hours, at the end of which a list of matters needing to be addressed had been put together. Maggie knew that there was no way she could escape joining Jack and Roy when they met the trawler owners.

Chapter 12

Maggie reached for the Daily Mail as it was being pushed through the letterbox. She smiled; they had made front-page headlines. A large photograph of the committee was spread across three columns of the paper. Underneath, in large bold letters, were the words: Maggie reaches for the sky. Now, the trawler owners must listen to what the women have to say... The cameraman had caught her waving her arm in the air; like Hitler, she thought. She was becoming a celebrity, not only in the press but also on the radio. One newscaster had likened her to Joan of Arc; small and fearless. But, this was not what Maggie wanted. She did not like being in the spotlight, but knew that it was inevitable. But, she was not fighting alone. The newspaper editors and the news broadcasters should advertise that fact more widely.

.The Daily Mail described the recent meeting of the committee as explosive. One after another, people had stood up and castigated the trawler owners for their criminal disregard for their crews' safety onboard their vessels; and also for their selfish lack of compassion for the bereaved families. Time and again, the matter of radio operators was brought up. Someone suggested that, perhaps, a mother ship could be based at the fishing grounds, which would then be in constant touch with the other vessels in the area. That way, the alarm could be raised quickly if contact was lost with a vessel for any length of time. The audience applauded him as he sat down.

The last paragraph of the article announced: Meetings have been scheduled over the next two or three weeks, between Anderson's, McKenzie's, Jack Lewis and Roy Morgan, Trade Union representatives, and Maggie Bell and her supporters. The trawler owners can no longer ignore the strength of feeling within the fishing community today.

'We **are** going to win,' Maggie Bell had insisted, when she was interviewed by Tim Dalton, a reporter from the *Daily Mail,* at the end of the meeting.

'My bet is definitely on her and her army of supporters,' Tim had concluded.

Maggie put the newspaper onto the table for Nora to read; she had gone to Jordan's at the top of the street. Martha was sitting in her chair as usual, rocking. She was smiling; it was unusual. Maggie sat down on a stool at her mother's feet. She liked to talk to her at some point every day; there was never any verbal response from her mother but, perhaps, one day… 'I don't know if you can hear me, mam, or understand what I'm saying, but I'm going to tell you, anyway, what I have been doing.'

She held her mother's hand gently in her own. Even though Martha had lost a lot of weight, her hands were still larger than her daughter's. Maggie took after Terry's side of the family; small frame and slender limbs.

'We're starting to get somewhere with the campaign, mam. I'm going to a meeting with Anderson's on Thursday with Pat, to try to make them listen to us. You remember Pat, don't you, mam? She's been my friend since we were little girls.'

Martha's eyes were vacant; not even a glimmer to indicate that her daughter's words had registered.

'I'm going to make those at the top pay for what they have done to our family, and to others, mam. I am going to fight to the bitter end and I am determined to win. Jack Lewis and Roy Morgan are going to be at the meeting, too.'

Martha's eyes seemed to flicker slightly; but it could have been in Maggie's imagination; seeing what she wanted to see. She heard the front door open. Nora was back. She kissed her mother on the cheek and then stood up.

She smiled. 'Hello, Auntie Nora.' Maggie's face became serious. 'What's the matter? What's wrong?'

'Probably nothing, lass, but there's a couple of newspaper reporters standing outside waiting to talk to you.'

'What about?'

'The campaign, of course; just a few words about your next move, they said.'

Maggie knew that there was no way she was going be rid of the men unless she went outside. 'I'd better see them otherwise they might frighten my mother. There's no way they are coming in here and upsetting her. I don't want them banging on the door, either.' As she made her way to the front door, she prepared herself for the coming ordeal. Once, again, she had to remind herself that the media was now a necessary part of her everyday life.

As soon as she opened the front door, Maggie was dazzled by flashing lights. She put her hands across her eyes. 'Turn them off or I'm going in.'

The two men put down their cameras immediately.

'What is it you want to know?' Maggie asked them, her eyes beginning to adjust to the light.

'Are you and your supporters planning to go to Downing Street, Maggie?'

'Everything's possible. If it's the only way to get things done quickly, then yes, we shall be marching on Downing Street. We are taking advice from Jack Lewis and Roy Morgan. But, at the end of the day, we are determined to get what we want, with or without the help of the Trade Unions.' As she said that, she felt guilty. 'But, we do appreciate all the help and support they can give us,' she added.

'Is it true that you were a secretary at McKenzie's when you started your campaign?'

Maggie tensed. 'I worked there, temporarily. The campaign did not get off the ground until after that. I cannot see why you have brought that up.'

'Kathleen McKenzie has told us that you were dismissed because of misconduct. Is that true? Are you trying to get back at the company for personal reasons?'

Maggie was furious. 'Kathleen McKenzie is a very vicious woman. To put the record straight, I was not dismissed. I left. As regards the campaign, I have lost my fiancée, my father and my brother to the sea. There are many more bereaved families in the city and many generations in the past have suffered the same fate. The fight is on behalf of all of them. Does that answer your question?'

'We are on your side, Maggie,' replied the reporter who had questioned her about McKenzie's.

'I have nothing else to say, at the moment, and must go in now. I have a very busy day ahead.'

'Working on the campaign?'

'No. It has nothing to do with that. It's a personal matter.'

'Fair enough, Maggie. We'll leave you be, then. Thanks and good luck.'

Closing the front door behind her, Maggie realized she was shaking. She walked into the kitchen as Nora came in from the front sitting room. 'That cow, Kathleen McKenzie, is trying to blacken my name, Auntie Nora.'

'I know. I opened a window slightly in the front room and was listening; being nosey. I wouldn't normally do something like that but I knew it was nothing private.' Nora put her arm around Maggie and made her sit down. 'She's going to be a hard one to fight, lass, but she can't win. There are too many people backing your campaign.'

'She is running the company with Paul, at the moment, because her husband is still in hospital. Paul is a kind and gentle person, Auntie Nora. I know that he could be persuaded to look at ways to improve safety on the company's ships but I don't feel he is strong enough to stand up to his mother. She doesn't care about the crews. I don't think she cares about anyone other than herself. Not even her husband. If he dies, I wonder who will be running the company, then. I bet it won't be Paul.'

'You paint a very nasty picture of her, Maggie. Perhaps, she's better for knowing.'

'Believe me, Auntie Nora, she is not a nice person. She looks upon people like us as dirt. There's no way she's going to give in easily.'

Maggie wondered which could be worse: sitting in close proximity to Paul at the meeting in less than two weeks' time, her heart racing, hands sweating; or sitting at the same table as Kathleen McKenzie, exposed to the woman's vicious tongue.

Chapter 13

Two o'clock, Thursday, 23rd September. Venue: the offices of Christopher Anderson and Brothers, St Andrew's Dock:

Present:

Christopher M Anderson	–	*Company Chairman*
David L Anderson	–	*Company Director*
Alan R Anderson	–	*Company Director*
Jack Lewis	–	*Rep. T.G.W.U.*
Roy Morgan	–	*Rep. T.G.W.U.*
Maggie Bell	–	*Rep. W.C.S.T.*
Pat Bell	–	*Rep. W.C.S.T.*

Before the meeting commenced, Mr Christopher Anderson demanded that the two Daily Mail reporters, who had followed the representatives into the room, should leave immediately. Jack Lewis told them to stay; if they were made to go, he and the rest of his supporters would leave also. He pointed out that Anderson's would be shown in the media to be most uncooperative, even before any discussions had taken place. Christopher Anderson acceded, reluctantly, seating himself in a huge leather chair behind the polished oak desk. His large broad frame fitted easily into its generous depths. His picture hung on the wall behind him; the word 'Chairman' had been carved into the brass plaque hanging below the frame. His brothers sat, one on either side of him, in comfortable but less sumptuous seats. They had offices elsewhere in the building, equally as plush as Christopher's. Their visitors sat in a small moon shape in front of the desk. The chairman reminded Maggie of the giant in Jack and the Beanstalk; big and threatening.

Christopher looked at his watch, then at Alan to his left.

'Have you another appointment, Mr Anderson?' Roy snapped.

'My brothers and I have a Board Meeting arranged for this afternoon, Roy, but we can spare you half an hour,' he replied, patronisingly.

'We had better get on then, hadn't we, Christopher?' Roy asked, sarcastically.

The chairman glared at him. But, he should have asked permission to use Roy's Christian name.

'Shall I begin?' suggested Jack, to break the ice, looking questioningly at all three brothers. Without waiting for an answer, he continued. 'The reason for the meeting today is to talk to you about the many concerns the fishing community have regarding safety on trawlers.' He looked at Christopher. 'You have already met Maggie and Pat Bell, I believe, and you do, of course, know Roy.'

Christopher was silent, his blue eyes steely and unfathomable.

Jack continued. 'At a meeting in the Victoria Hall recently, organised by Maggie and her supporters, several suggestions were put forward which we all feel could help to reduce the number of fatalities and accidents onboard fishing vessels.

David Anderson interrupted him. 'You seem to be singling out this company more than any others. Why is that?'

'I must correct you there, Mr Anderson,' snapped Maggie. 'We have a meeting arranged with McKenzie's for next week. The only reason you appear to have been highlighted is that the *St Lawrence*, the last vessel to be lost, was one of your ships. There is a strong feeling in the community, including amongst members of your own staff that you waited far too long before investigating why nothing had been heard from the ship for nearly two weeks. That sounds like gross neglect to me, Mr Anderson. Criminal, in fact.' Maggie resisted the temptation to use his Christian name.

'You have already been given the reasons for that,' David Anderson snapped. 'The ship had a faulty radio. We tried very hard to contact it, with no avail.'

'Obviously, not hard enough, Mr Anderson,' answered Maggie.

'You insisted to the very end that there was nothing to worry about,' said Pat, angrily. 'Do you all sleep easily in your beds at night?' she asked, looking at each of the three brothers in turn.

'I'm sure I can speak for us all. We sleep very well, thank you,' replied Alan, flippantly. But, the three company directors were looking increasingly uncomfortable, their eyes straying occasionally to the two reporters who were sitting at the back of the room near to the door; their pencils were speeding across the blank sheets of their notebooks, leaving a written language, which only those who were familiar with the squiggles and lines could understand. Two pairs of eyes rose occasionally to observe the heated debate.

'Let's keep to the matter in hand, shall we,' said Jack, quickly. 'Bringing personalities into the discussion will not help anyone.' He looked at Christopher. 'One of the suggestions made was that perhaps a vessel could be made available at the fishing grounds, which would act as a kind of Mother Ship; a hospital and rescue vessel. I know this would cost a lot of money but we are talking here about men's lives. We would like you to give serious consideration to this matter.'

'We shall certainly look into it carefully but we need to be given time to do so,' replied David Anderson.

'Our men don't always have the luxury of time. Ships go down in minutes,' answered Pat.

David Anderson ignored her remark and continued. 'The kind of vessel you are talking about is not currently available to the fishing fleet. And, it would be very expensive to provide.'

'Here we go again,' shouted Maggie, her cheeks painted an angry red. 'Everything always comes down to money,' She stood up, shaking uncontrollably. 'Our men die to line your pockets, feather your nests. We are talking here about wives becoming widows, children left fatherless. Have you no pity at all for them?'

'Sit down, Maggie,' insisted Jack. 'Let's keep calm.'

'No, I won't sit down. I'm sick of hearing their excuses.'

'Give Mr Anderson a chance to talk, Maggie. Let's not jump to conclusions,' Roy said.

She sat down reluctantly.

'Will you please look at the suggestion for a Mother Ship after the meeting?' Roy asked, looking hard at the three brothers.

'Yes, we'll do that,' replied the men, nodding at each other in agreement.

'But, we cannot promise anything in the near future,' added the company chairman. Never before had he chaired a meeting such as this. Two women facing him across the table who were not only intending to be heard, but also to get what they wanted. He looked more confident at Board Meetings.

'The next thing we want to talk about, Christopher, is the importance of a fully trained radio operator on board ship.' Jack was following the same pattern as Roy; Christian names to be used; the chairman had dictated the pattern. 'At an informal meeting yesterday between myself, Roy and the women's committee, it was suggested that a safety check should be made of all equipment prior to a trawler leaving port. As you know, the crew of the *Lexicon* refused to sail last week because they were not happy with the lifejackets onboard ship. It is not one of your ships, I know, but next week it could be. If a ship doesn't sail, the men lose money; but you do, too. So, I'm sure you would agree that it would be in all our interests for you to look at this matter urgently.'

The three directors made no reply.

Maggie whispered into Jack's ear, 'Don't forget about the meeting in London.'

'I was coming to that,' he replied. He turned his attention back to the stony-faced men at the other side of the desk. 'As you all know, a meeting has been arranged for next Monday at the offices of the Agriculture and Fisheries Ministry. Myself, and my three colleagues here, will be attending. A report on that meeting will be circulated to the Hull trawler owners soon after our return.'

There was a gentle tap at the door then a slim young woman entered. She walked across to Christopher and whispered in his ear. His face paled. As the woman left the room, he looked first at his brothers then at Jack. He cleared his throat, nervously. 'It would appear that the *Sardinia* has gone down off Norway with the loss of all hands. I can only express my deep sorrow for all the families concerned.'

'And ours, of course,' said Alan, looking totally shocked.

'It's dreadful,' added David. 'I'm very sorry.'

'But it was not one of ours. It belonged to Walton's,' Christopher pointed out.

Maggie was stunned; boiling rage erupted inside her. 'And that makes it okay, does it? Why am I getting a feeling of déjà vu again?' She stood up, banging her chair noisily against the wall as she did so. She made her way to the door. Pat followed her.

'I hope you both have a good time in London,' Christopher Anderson called after them.

Maggie opened the front door and took a step backwards. 'What on earth has happened to you, Alice?'

'Can I come in, Maggie?"

A few minutes later, seated on the comfortable but sagging settee in the Bell's kitchen, a cup of tea held shakily in her hand, Alice explained in graphic detail the brutal beating she had endured at her husband's hands on his return from a trip to Iceland.

The moment Ray had walked through the front door and into the living room, Alice's whole body had stiffened; her husband's face was set, his eyes wild and furious; he had been drinking. Alice knew immediately that he had been told about her involvement in the women's campaign. She had expected an angry reaction from him but not one so violent. She was used to his occasional physical attacks after he had been drinking but she knew that this time there was far worse to come.

'When I landed, every bastard on the dock was sneering at me. You've made a bloody laughing stock out of me, woman, and I'm not bloody well putting up with it.'

Whilst Ray had been away, Alice had spent a great deal of time petitioning, talking to people in the community, who did not normally have a good word to say about skippers, their wives and families. As the time went by, she had felt increasingly confident that she was winning them over to her side. She had been too busy to worry about her husband's reaction to what she had been doing, when he returned home.

'So you know. Who told you?'

'Some bugger sent a message a few days ago, anonymously. I don't know where it came from and I don't bloody care. What does matter is that you're not having anything more to do with the carryings on with that lot of common tarts. Your place is in the home, not on the streets waving a bloody banner. You're a skipper's wife, not a stinking deckhand's.'

Then the blows had started, first to Alice's face, then to her body. Her right arm was wrenched sideways as she tried to escape the beating, which she had known would come and had dreaded. Her doll-like figure had been no match for her husband's solid five-feet ten-inch frame; and his strong hands as they circled her throat.

Alice paused, weeping, as she relayed her story through torn lips and a broken front tooth. Maggie took the tea out of her hand and put an arm around her friend's shoulders. 'I'm so sorry, Alice. Perhaps, it would be better if you left the campaigning to the rest of us. You've done a lot of good work and I'm sure that nobody would want you to continue if this is how you are going to end up. Your husband has, obviously, got a very violent temper. He could kill you next time.'

Alice wiped her eyes. 'No, Maggie, there is no way I am going to give in to him,' she said adamantly. 'I am going to stand my ground. I'm not going to be the little woman tied to the kitchen sink anymore, making sure that his meals are on the table every time he comes in from the pub. I'll continue to live up to my responsibilities at home, within reason, and for the time being, but I've changed. Women have been kept under their men's thumbs for far too long. It's time for us to let them see that we are not just skivvies in the home.'

'I completely agree with you, Alice.'

'We have a right to some respect and to be able to have our say,' continued Alice, becoming more and more animated, her painful injuries temporarily forgotten. 'It doesn't make the men appear weak if we stand up to them. That's not what we are trying to do. We are not challenging their manhood and it is time that they realised what the campaign is really about.'

'I think we've all changed, Alice. The trouble is that the men are finding it difficult to accept that we are fighting for them, when they know they should have done it for themselves a long time ago.'

'You're quite right, lass.'

Maggie stared in shock at Martha. 'Mam, did you say something?'

Martha's face was, as usual, vacant.

'Am I hearing things, Alice?'

'No, Maggie, your mother said, "You're quite right, lass." I heard it as clear as a bell,' Alice confirmed. 'Perhaps, she's getting better.'

'It would be wonderful if that were true.' Maggie walked across to Martha. 'How are you, mam?'

There was no reply

'I must go now, Maggie,' Alice said, standing up, straightening her skirt as she did so.

'You don't have to go. You're welcome to stay.'

'Thanks, Maggie, but I'm feeling a lot better now. And, Ray will be sleeping off the booze. But, he had better not lay a finger on me, ever again. If he does, I shall leave him. To be honest, I've been thinking about doing that for a very long time. I don't love him anymore, Maggie.'

'I had no idea, Alice. I'm very sorry.'

'There was no reason why you should have known, Maggie. It isn't something you want to broadcast, is it?' Alice walked towards the door. She turned. 'You'll be having a meeting with McKenzie's next week, won't you?'

Maggie's heart lurched.

'And, there's the meeting in London on Monday,' Alice continued. 'Let me know what happened, won't you? Things are looking really promising for us now.'

'Everyone will be kept up to date,' Maggie answered, trying to keep her voice steady.

———————

As Maggie approached the factory gates, she felt Pat grip her arm, encouragingly. This was the first time she had been on McKenzie's premises since the day she had walked out from her job as secretary; thus denying Kathleen McKenzie the pleasure of sacking her. The memory of that last furious encounter with the woman she knew hated her, still remained with her, vividly.

Jack and Roy were walking a few feet in front of them; Maggie had made sure of that; she did not want to be the first one into the building, even though she knew her way about the offices. Soon she would be sitting at the same table as Paul; it would be hard for her to be in the same room as him, sitting face to face across a desk.

She would also have to face Kathleen, his mother, who would most certainly be at the meeting, if only to make Maggie squirm. She would be sitting with the patient sobriety of a hungry vulture, eyes dark and malevolent, ready to pounce and destroy her victim at every opportunity; gnawing and stripping away at the last vestiges of what made Maggie the person she was. She would probably arrive first at the meeting table; another cruel tactic to demoralise Maggie.

'Remember why we are here, ' Pat prompted her friend, by digging her in the ribs. 'Don't let Paul or his mother get in the way of that. Think about the lads.'

A few minutes later, seated in the company's Board Room, the meeting was ready to commence. On one side of the long leather-topped table sat Jack, Roy, Maggie and Pat. Opposite them were Kathleen, Paul, and a very attractive blonde girl holding a notebook and pencil.

Maggie felt a stab of jealousy; inferiority. Her lemon blouse and dark green skirt, which had felt smart and pretty earlier that morning, now felt dowdy. She had studied her reflection in the mirror, carefully, before she left home, knowing that she would be under scrutiny from Kathleen. And, she had had to admit to herself, that she wanted to look her best in front of Paul; she was entitled to her pride. Now, as she compared herself with the young woman next to Paul, her efforts seemed to have been wasted. The pretty, blonde secretary was a picture of confidence and elegance; navy-blue suit, white blouse, and a neat string of pearls, giving a finishing touch to the v-neck.

But, there had been no need for Maggie to worry. The sunlight through the office windows was playing upon the copper-red tones in her hair. The thick curling strands had been combed high at the back of her head and wound into a coil, accentuating her fine bone structure, especially when viewed from the side. Her make-up was light; a touch of pink blusher to her cheeks, her lips painted a delicate shade of coral pink. She suddenly became aware that Paul was looking at her, smiling. She blushed and turned away.

'You all know my son, of course, and this is Amanda, his secretary, who will be taking the minutes.' Kathleen McKenzie smiled at the girl, then at the visitors, her eyes lingering on Maggie; spiteful, speaking volumes. 'Amanda is excellent at her work. Her father is a Member of Parliament,' she said, still looking at Maggie.

Pat dug her friend sharply in the ribs to remind her of her priorities.

Paul looked at his mother, angrily. She gave no indication that she had noticed; there was no sign that she even cared. He took over before she could say anything else. 'I would like to declare this meeting open and to welcome you all here today to discuss your concerns regarding safety on trawlers and to look at ways for improvement.'

'Not specifically McKenzie's vessels,' Kathleen said, sharply.

'Our being here today does not signify that yours or any other particular company is being targeted,' retorted Jack.. 'The matter of safety involves every company and the fishermen themselves. To this end, numerous meetings have been taking place both locally and in London.'

'Have you had time to put together a report on what happened at the meeting with the Ministry of Agriculture and Fisheries and the Board of Trade?' Paul asked.

'Yes, I have; a brief one. The delegation was made up of myself, Roy, Maggie and Pat, and Roger Horncastle and Andrew Mainprize, both local Members of Parliament who have joined our fight. Donald Brown and Leonard Peterson, ministers for Board of Trade and Agriculture and Fisheries, met us at the Houses of Parliament. Our meeting was both cordial and productive. Maggie and Pat presented to the two ministers a petition of over ten thousand signatures that the Women's Committee had collected, and also a list of suggestions, which could effectively make up a charter covering all areas of safety at sea. The ministers took them away and promised to come back to us with their comments, as soon as they can. We shall, of course, let you know their response, when we hear from them. I will now hand you over to Maggie, who will go over those suggestions with you.'

Maggie tried consciously to slow down her heartbeat; to not look at either Paul or his mother. She was as good as the McKenzie's, so why should she feel inferior? But, the fact remained that she did; even more so, when sitting opposite Amanda, with her perfect looks and perfect dress-sense. She struggled to remain calm and try not to let her voice shake. 'As Jack said, our meeting in London, with the ministers of the Board of Trade and Agriculture and Fisheries, was very successful, far more than we would have hoped. The ministers listened to what we had to say. We were never talked down to because we are women.' Maggie caught Kathleen's eye and was unable to stop herself from blushing. She was angry for reacting. But, it made her voice stronger. 'Pat and I were treated the same as the men. We weren't laughed at. Nobody told us that we were only fishermen's wives tied to the kitchen sink. And, as Jack said, both the ministers agreed to look at our suggestions and report back to us.' She paused briefly to take a sip of water from the glass in front of her. A thought flashed through her mind. Had Kathleen poisoned it? She felt her eyes twinkle, then immediately became serious again. It was too brief a moment for anyone else to have noticed. But, she was gaining confidence as she spoke. 'The Women's Committee are demanding that a vessel should never leave port without a full crew and, most importantly, a fully qualified radio operator; there should be regular twelve-hour contact between trawlers and their base; safety equipment should be checked and improved, if necessary, before leaving port; medical ships should be provided at the fishing grounds. There should be a minimum age agreed for boys working on vessels at sea and adequate training given to those taken on. And, young boys should never be allowed to sail during the winter months. Fishing off the north coast of Iceland in the winter should be banned. Finally, a union representative with sole responsibility for the men's safety should be aboard every ship when it leaves port. The ministers in London supported every point we put forward.' She sat down, her heart banging against her chest; she felt drained.

Kathleen sprang up like a furious feline protecting its young. ' There is no way that fishing off Iceland in the winter can be banned. Nor, will this company allow a union representative to be onboard ship every time a ship sails. It is not necessary. The financial repercussions would be enormous. It would not only affect the trawler owners, it would also mean that men's jobs would be lost.' She looked at Maggie. 'Is that what you want?' she asked her, furiously. 'This is your doing, miss. You're not worried about the men, you're only interested in getting your face on the front of the Hull Daily Mail.' Water was dribbling down the sides of her mouth.

Maggie stood up again and faced her enemy, her green eyes ablaze. 'I knew we would get nowhere with you. But you have shown everyone here what you are really like. You are a selfish, mercenary woman without compassion. You are the one who does not care about the men, not me. It's money, money, money, with you.' Maggie was in full flow and she would allow nothing to stop her tirade. 'Tell me something. Every time one of your vessels leaves for the Arctic, do you shed any tears? Are you anxious about the horrendous weather conditions our men will encounter? Do you worry in your bed that they may not come back? No. You only think about lining your pockets. You have no conscience. Well, I'm sorry if it is going to upset your comfortable existence, but conditions onboard all trawlers, including yours, are going to change dramatically; for the better. Now that another ship has been lost with all hands, not one of your ships, I know, but a trawler nevertheless, the Government are taking our complaints seriously. You and your lot will soon have no choice but to give in. You've lost the fight. Accept defeat gracefully, if you can.'

Pat immediately stood up, clapping loudly and beaming at her friend. 'Well done, Maggie. It's been us against them but we're winning.'

Roy took hold of Maggie's arm. 'Sit down both of you. We haven't finished yet,' he said.

'Oh, but we have,' snapped Kathleen. 'Certainly as far as I am concerned.' She picked up her papers then stormed towards the door. She turned and looked at Maggie, again. The deep hate festering inside her was blatantly obvious. 'You haven't heard the last of this. You're nothing but a common slut.' The walls vibrated as she slammed the door behind her.

The tears came. Maggie was unable to hold them back. Roy patted her arm. 'She's gone now, Maggie, so calm down.'

Paul was visibly upset. 'I can only apologise for my mother, Maggie. Her behaviour, and what she said to you, was inexcusable.' He turned to his secretary. 'Could you please get us another jug of water, Amanda?'

She stood up and left the room.

'If it makes you feel any better, Maggie, I think you and your committee have done an excellent job in listing the problems of safety which need to be addressed,' Paul said. He looked at the rest of the group. 'As you all know, my father is seriously ill in hospital and, for the time being, my mother and I are dealing with company matters. I will talk to her regarding the suggestions that have been put forward and I am sure that, after she has had time to cool down and think, she will take a positive attitude towards them.'

'It is not particularly important to us what your mother thinks.' Jack pointed out. 'At the end of the day, if Government ministers are on our side, and I am sure they are, there will be nothing she or anyone else can do to avoid significant changes being made throughout the fishing industry. It will be costly but what price can be put on a man's head?'

Paul nodded in agreement. 'If you would like to leave a copy of all your suggestions, I will look at them and come back to you shortly.' He looked at Maggie. 'I can only say, once again, Maggie, that I am very sorry for the way my mother has treated you today.'

Maggie could not bring herself to look at him. She knew that her eyes were swollen, her cheeks an angry red; she felt a mess. Amanda looked embarrassed at what she had witnessed; but still in control and immaculate.

'I am afraid I shall have to leave now,' Paul announced. 'But we shall all meet again soon. By the time my mother and I have perused your suggestions, you will probably have heard from the ministers at Whitehall. Thank you all for coming.' He gathered up his papers and stood up to leave. He smiled at Maggie, sadly. She handed him the list he wanted then he left the room with Amanda. Moments later, the rest of the group followed them. Outside the offices, Jack and Roy announced that they had business to deal with elsewhere; they promised they would be in touch with Maggie and Pat within the next few days.

As they walked arm in arm across the factory yard, Maggie saw Paul standing near his car. He called her name. Then she saw Keith walking towards her. Paul had seen him, too; he climbed into his car and left.

'You look upset,' Keith said to Maggie, as he joined her and Pat. He was studying her tear-stained face intently. His eyes strayed towards Paul's car as it went through the gates. 'Was it something *he* said? Or was it his bloody mother?'

'It was nothing, Keith,' Maggie replied. 'I had a flaming row at the end of the meeting with Kathleen McKenzie but I gave as good as I got, didn't I, Pat?'

'You certainly did. Kathleen McKenzie's face was a picture. She stormed out of the office. Paul apologised to Maggie.'

Keith's eyes narrowed. 'You are not going to let him get round you, I hope.'

'Of course I'm not. What do you take me for?' Maggie snapped.

'His mother was awful to her,' Pat explained. 'Paul looked very embarrassed.'

'Let's talk about something else,' Maggie said.

———————

Three weeks later, as Maggie led the way into Victoria Hall with Pat and Alice immediately behind her, they were met with a standing ovation. The atmosphere was electric; different from the last meeting in the hall – just as powerful but this time with hope, not anger. Everybody was standing; children on chairs. And, there were many more men at this meeting than the last time; all squashed amongst the women and their offspring. 'Maggie. Maggie. We want Maggie,' came the calls. Children's voices went unheeded amidst the rapturous applause around them.

This meeting had been arranged to update the community on the group's trip to Westminster and the meetings with the trawler owners. As soon as the committee were seated, Jack turned to Maggie and said, 'Come on, lass. Stand up and let them see and hear you. It's what you deserve.'

'This isn't only about me, Jack, it's been a joint effort.'

'We want Maggie. We want Maggie.'

At last, she stood up, overwhelmed and embarrassed by the strength of the people's reception. How many years had she waited for this? How long had she wished she could tell the fishing community of Hull that things would be better soon for the trawlermen? Her eyes were brimming over as she looked out on the sea of faces in front of her,

her embarrassment now disappearing. In it's place, an overpowering feeling of intense happiness. She opened her mouth to say something but the words would not come out.

'Come on, Maggie, they're waiting to hear what you have to say,' Pat insisted.

Jack left his seat and banged hard onto the table. He lifted his hand. 'Please, everybody, be quiet or you won't be able to hear Maggie speak.' The audience became quiet, immediately.

Maggie cleared her throat. 'Today is not about me. It is about all of us. Recently, the city was hit, yet again, with the tragic news that another trawler; the *Sardinia,* had gone down with the loss of all members of its crew. I do not need to tell you all of the deep sadness I, and my friends here with me today, feel for the families and loved ones left behind. Would you all please bow your heads in a minute's silence, to remember the twenty-two brave young men who are no longer with us.'

The hall could have been any empty church on a weekday; the silence was only broken by the whimpering of a young child and the gentle crying of a woman; perhaps one of the recently bereaved.

Maggie broke the silence. 'Thank you everybody. I can now tell you, categorically, that today is a day of hope for our community. At last, our fight is being recognised by the Government, for the just cause it is. The trawler owners are losing their power.'

The audience roared, clapped, booed. Jack stood up again, smiling, and banged on the table. 'Will you all please try to control your enthusiasm; otherwise, you will not hear what is being said. There will be plenty of time at the end of the meeting to have your say and show your appreciation.' Once again, everybody obeyed. 'Continue, Maggie.'

'Thank you Jack.' Maggie turned to the audience. 'Hundreds of trawlermen have lost their lives at sea, many of them needlessly, over many years. Others have been seriously injured, many not able to work again, whilst the owners feathered their nests. Blood money, it was.' Again, she was interrupted by cheering and shouting from the audience. She waited until they had quietened down. 'We knew in our hearts that this could not be right. Of course, ships will still go down occasionally because of severe weather conditions, taking the crews with them. Of course, men will be seriously injured, lose limbs and fingers onboard ship, whilst doing what fishermen have to do. But, we have always believed that some situations can be avoided or, at least, made safer. Now, with the Government on our side, the trawler owners will have to make every effort they can to provide safer working conditions onboard their vessels. This will give our fishermen a better chance of survival and minimise the risk of accidents. Your husbands, your sons, your lovers are entitled to this. We truly believe that we now have hope. Our luck has changed. Thank you everyone for your support.'

Maggie sat down, her ears ringing from the noise of people shouting, calling her name; it was deafening. People were stampeding in the aisles, some of them trying to reach the platform, others hoping to make their way out as quickly as they could. Katy was sitting in the front row looking bewildered. Pat went down the platform steps and pushed her way through the crowd milling around her. She lifted her daughter and managed to rejoin the rest of the committee on the stage. Cameras were flashing, as the reporters at the back of the hall prepared to wind-up and rush back to the Mail offices to catch the next edition.

'I'm so proud of you, Maggie,' whispered Pat, tears running down her cheeks. 'You've gained so much confidence, it amazes me.'

'Hello, Auntie Maggie.'

Maggie looked down at her Godchild then stroked her satin-skinned cheek. 'Hello, Katie, I hope your daddy has been watching this afternoon.'

'He was. I saw him. He was smiling.'

'I'm sure he was, sweetheart,' Maggie replied. She turned to Pat. 'It hasn't only been me who has achieved our aims, or most of them, Pat. Everyone on the committee, including Jack and Roy, has done their share. And, at what cost, when you look at Alice?'

Pat looked at their friend sitting nearby. Alice's bruises were now a yellowish shade of green, her lips not so swollen. The absence of a front tooth was noticeable only when she smiled. She had plenty to be pleased about today, even though her marriage was over. All her work and support on behalf of the committee had come to fruition. She was a survivor like the rest of the women on the Hessle Road..

Jack stood up and hammered loudly on the table. 'I would like you all, before you leave, to sing *Eternal Father Strong to Save.*'

A handful of people continued on their way out of the hall. The majority stopped in their tracks. There was no piano; no orchestra. But, the voices of the people swelled to the ceiling and beyond, a powerful outpouring of community spirit, love, compassion and friendship. Nobody, nor anything, could take those precious moments away from them. They could look to the future now with hope. There would always be loss of life and limb, but at least now there would be some protection for the men.

Maggie sat at the kitchen table holding a cup of tea. She gave a contented sigh; she could now concentrate on other things, her own needs. All the hard work that she and her friends had undertaken on behalf of the men had been worthwhile. Some safety measures had already taken place on the fishing vessels and the docks. Government officials, together with other echelons of society, including the trawler owners, were now in consultations regarding other important improvements that needed to be made.

A weather reporting ship was to be stationed off the coast of Iceland. Skippers had to take shelter in bad weather, when advised to do so, and a modern trawler was to be equipped to act as a hospital ship. A new de-icing device was being tried out, which would be attached to a ship's main mast; it used compressed air to crack ice as it formed. The Board of Trade was undertaking a blanket investigation into all aspects of safety on trawlers. Dr Andrew Parkinson, who had held positions in the Royal Navy at the most senior levels and had had extensive experience in the field of health risks and safety onboard ship, had been appointed as the committee's chief advisor. The trawler owners tried to block the appointment because Dr Parkinson was known to be a formidable opponent, vociferous in his criticism of the poor standards of safety that had been allowed to prevail over many years. The trawler owners' attempts were defeated.

Another argument had developed when the trade unions had demanded representation onboard all vessels when they left port, to monitor safety levels; a point that had already enraged the trawler owners, once before. On this occasion, the trade unions had lost; the owners had refused to give way.

'It could cause mutiny. Skippers would no longer be in charge of their own vessels,' Kathleen McKenzie had insisted. She had later taken up the issue with her son. 'You are like your father; not hard enough to run a business. Take a leaf out of my book, son.'

'I've no intention of doing that, mother. Your way rarely gets good results. You were lucky this time.'

———————————

Maggie put her empty cup onto the table. She suddenly felt deflated, like a balloon that had been flying high and free when, for some unknown reason, it suddenly bursts. Over the past few weeks, she had put all her energies into the campaign. Now it was over. She, and the rest of the committee, had fought hard and won. She could now leave the betting shop and find herself a full-time job in an office. Her engagement ring would soon return to where it belonged. So, why should she suddenly feel so empty?

———

'Hello, Maggie, can I come in?'

Maggie stared at Paul. Without any argument, she led him into the kitchen. She wanted to ask him why he had come but she was speechless. She had not seen him since the meeting at McKenzie's over a month ago.

'You probably have not heard, Maggie, but Kenny is very ill in hospital. I've come to ask you if you'll visit him. He's been asking for you.'

Maggie gave a swift intake of breath; her body tensed. 'What is the matter with him? How is he?'

'The doctors thought he had polio but, thankfully, they were wrong. He is still quite ill. Twice a day, the nurses get him out of bed to exercise his legs.'

'I am so sorry, Paul. I had no idea. Of course, I'll visit him.' She paused. 'But, what will your mother say?'

'It has nothing to do with her. We go our separate ways nowadays. You will, of course, know that my father died two weeks ago and that I am running the company now. That was what he wanted. It was in his will.'

'Yes, I saw the report in the Daily Mail. You must miss him very much. He was a very kind man. It must be extremely difficult for you, at the moment. You're going through an awful time and I don't know what to say.'

'There is no need to say anything, Maggie. All I ask is that you come with me to see Kenny. I'm sure it will help him to get better quicker. I am going to the hospital this afternoon. I could pick you up at two o'clock, if that's convenient?'

Maggie bit her lip. She was expecting Keith to come to the house at that time. She did not want any trouble but she needed to see Kenny. He was more important.

'Is there a problem, Maggie? If there is, I can take you another time, perhaps tomorrow might be more convenient for you,' Paul offered.

'No, there isn't a problem for this afternoon, Paul. I'll meet you at the top of the street. It will save you some time.'

He looked at her curiously but didn't question her. He stood up. 'I'll leave you now. I'm sure you have things to do.' He looked across at Martha. She smiled at him. He looked at her in amazement.

'My mother seems to be more aware of things, lately,' explained Maggie. 'She even talks occasionally. Nora takes her out in a wheelchair every day, providing the weather's reasonable.'

Maggie did not tell Paul that it now seemed Martha had been aware of what was going on around her for some time. Delayed shock, the doctor had said, due to losing her husband and both of her sons, at separate times; it had to come out sometime and now, hopefully, she was getting better.

Maggie led Paul to the front door. 'I'll see you later.' she said, as he was leaving. Then she remembered something. 'I didn't offer you a drink. I didn't think. I'm sorry, Paul.' She blushed with embarrassment.

'I haven't time for one today, Maggie. So don't worry about it. Perhaps, you'll offer me one another time.' Paul smiled at her; that smile that haunted her every night as she lay in her bed trying to get to sleep, wrapped in the comforting warmth of her patchwork quilt. She closed the front door, having watched him walk to the end of the terrace, where he had left his car. She had longed for him to kiss her when he left; he would never know that.

'I like him, Maggie.'

Maggie looked across at Martha. 'So do I, mam; too much.'

It seemed very strange walking down the hospital ward by Paul's side; yet, for some reason, it did not feel wrong.

'Maggie. Maggie.' A small voice travelled towards them. She tensed. If only the words could have been, 'Mummy. Mummy.'

As she approached Kenny's bedside, tears came to Maggie's eyes. A white face, framed by a mop of blonde curls, was looking up at her, smiling. Without hesitation she stooped and kissed his soft, warm cheek, then gently feathered her hand across his forehead.

'I'll find us a couple of chairs,' Paul told her, after bending down to kiss his son.

'I want to go home, Maggie.'

'Yes, I know, sweetheart.' It was a word she had only used rarely in the past. 'How are you feeling? You've given everyone a fright, you know. You've been so poorly.'

'I'm getting better now.'

'I do hope so.'

Kenny leant cautiously across the bed and reached for a glass of water that was standing on the small cabinet next to him. Maggie's eyes were momentarily glued to the bare skin; exposed when his pyjama top had parted from the bottom. It was there; the mark. 'Let me hold that for you,' she said quickly, noticing that Kenny's hand was shaking. Her heart was racing.

At that moment, Paul returned with the chairs. He sat down next to Maggie. She felt herself flinch slightly as a surge of warmth raced through her body. He smiled at her. Perhaps he hadn't noticed the movement; or, perhaps, he had and was amused. But, Maggie saw no evidence of this in his eyes.

The visit was brief; half an hour. That was the hospital's rule. One half-hour every day, in the afternoon but not on a Thursday; that was when the doctors visited the patients. Matron's menacing figure appeared at the end of the long ward. The time was precisely three o'clock; not a minute before, nor a minute after. She shook a large iron bell, sadistically. It was so loud that it could, originally, have been made for the battlefield or a prison yard.

'Time, everyone, please.' Her deep, strong voice, that could have been mistaken for a man's, travelled down the ward.

Maggie sighed. The time had gone so quickly. She struggled to keep calm as she bent to kiss Kenny goodbye..

'You will come to see me again, won't you Maggie?'

'Of course, I will.'

'Tomorrow?'

'No, I can't, I'm sorry. But, perhaps later in the week, if that's okay with your daddy.' Maggie looked at Paul.

'I'll bring you whenever you wish,' he replied. He turned to Kenny. 'Say thank you to Maggie for coming.'

'Thank you, Maggie.'

Paul kissed his son goodbye then walked up the ward next to Maggie. He took hold of her hand. 'When are you going to accept that I love you and want to marry you?' he whispered.

Maggie did not answer. But, nor did she release her hand. They made their way out of the hospital and walked across the grounds to Paul's car. He helped her into the passenger seat then walked around the front of the car to the driver's side. Soon after they set off, Maggie realised that they were travelling in the wrong direction to her home; yet she remained silent. She felt as if she was in a different world, a timewarp, where she had no control over of what was happening to her.

At last, they came to the open country on the outskirts of the city. In a quiet deserted lane, Paul turned off the engine and faced her. 'Please put me out of my misery and say you'll marry me, Maggie. It doesn't matter to me that I run a trawling company and you're a secretary.'

'I haven't been a secretary for quite a while,' Maggie replied sarcastically, although she was smiling slightly. 'Your mother sacked me, don't you remember? You were there.'

'Yes, I do remember and I wish I had done something to stop her at the time. I wasn't strong enough then, Maggie, but I've changed. She has gone to live with my sister in Wiltshire. We don't have any contact.'

Maggie thought about what it would be like if her and Martha no longer talked to, or saw, each other. Things were getting better at home. Martha was improving both physically and mentally, although there was still a long way to go. But, Maggie would always try to be there for her; with the help of Nora, who seemed to have boundless energy and never complained.

'If you married me, you would be with Kenny all the time, Maggie; not only now and again. He loves you, just as I do. And, after all, you are his birth mother.'

Maggie stared at him. 'You know,' she said, not knowing what else to say.

'Yes, I do, Maggie. When Sara and I adopted him, we had no idea who his parents were. As you know, Sara died from an asthmatic attack some time ago. She had no idea who Kenny's real mother was but she loved him as much as I did; and I still do.'

'How did you find out?' Maggie was crying.

'Unbeknown to me, my mother spent a lot of time and money after Kenny's adoption, bribing people for information, until finally she was shown a copy of his birth certificate, which named you and Andy, a fisherman, as his biological parents. That has been the main reason my mother hates you, Maggie. Your work with the campaign added to that. She became your enemy, about a year ago. I could never understand why she treated you the way she did.'

'Did your father know?' whispered Maggie.

'Yes, but not until his health started to fail. He was never strong enough to stand-up to her and he never told me that he knew. I wish he had.'

'Why did your mother eventually tell you? She must have realised that it could bring us closer together, if you really loved me,' Maggie pointed out.

'It was when she knew that she could no longer fight you and also that she had lost control of the company. The words poured out. I know that changes need to be made regarding safety on our trawlers and I respect that and will co-operate fully with the authorities. Mind you, I could do with a new secretary.' Paul was laughing now.

'Where's Amanda?'

'She left.'

'Oh, why was that?'

'She didn't like my mother. I can't believe that, can you, Maggie?' Paul was laughing.

'Does Kenny know who I really am?'

'No, but he has always known he was adopted. He'll be over the moon when we tell him,' replied Paul.

'I wonder if he will call me mummy.' Maggie was thoughtful for a moment then told Paul the story of the caul that had been wrapped around Kenny's head when he was born. She could now, at last, return it to it's owner.'

'I know things are not going to be easy for us, perhaps for a very long time, Maggie. But, things are changing dramatically in the fishing industry, in part due to you. We are all going to have to accept changes and compromises; the fishermen and the trawler owners have to learn to work together. I will always be there for you, Maggie, whatever the future might hold for us, I can promise you that. We love each other and it is all that really matters. Don't you agree?'

Maggie looked at him, her deep green eyes wet and shining. 'I hope so, Paul. I do hope so.'

THE END

About the Author

This is Eileen's second book to be published, the first being an *Anthology of Yorkshire Humour*. She is now working on another book, again based around the fishing community of Hull. It follows the lives of two local lads, both Hull trawlermen.

Eileen has been runner-up and highly commended in internet competitions. She has also had articles published in America, the last one being about the life of William Wilberforce, which entailed many weeks, if not months, of research. She was a runner-up in a N.A.W.G. competition for a ten-minute play.

Printed in the United Kingdom
by Lightning Source UK Ltd.
107463UKS00001B/31-39